MW01615196

Unlikely
SEASON

AN AMISH CHRISTMAS STORY

JENNIFER
SPREDEMANN

Published in Indiana by *Blessed Publishing*.
www.jenniferspredemann.com

All Scripture quotations are taken from the *King James Version* of the *Holy Bible*.

Cover design by *iCreate Designs* ©
Formatting by *Polgarus Studio*

ISBN: 978-1-940492-91-9
10 9 8 7 6 5 4 3 2 1

Get a FREE Amish story as my thank you gift when you sign up for my newsletter here: www.jenniferspredemann.com

BOOKS by JENNIFER SPREDEMANN

AMISH BY ACCIDENT TRILOGY
Amish by Accident
*Englisch on Purpose (*Prequel to *Amish by Accident)*
*Christmas in Paradise (*Sequel to *Amish by Accident*)
(co-authored with Brandi Gabriel)

AMISH SECRETS SERIES
An Unforgivable Secret - Amish Secrets 1
A Secret Encounter - Amish Secrets 2
A Secret of the Heart - Amish Secrets 3
An Undeniable Secret - Amish Secrets 4
A Secret Sacrifice - Amish Secrets 5 (co-authored
with Brandi Gabriel)
A Secret of the Soul - Amish Secrets 6
A Secret Christmas – Amish Secrets 2.5 (co-authored
with Brandi Gabriel)

KING FAMILY SAGA (AMISH ROMANCES)
An Amish Reward (Isaac)
An Amish Deception (Jacob)
An Amish Honor (Joseph)
An Amish Blessing (Ruth)
An Amish Betrayal (David)

AMISH COUNTRY BRIDES

The Trespasser (Amish Country Brides)
The Heartbreaker (Amish Country Brides)
The Charmer (Amish Country Brides)
The Drifter (Amish Country Brides)
The Giver (Amish Country Brides Christmas)
The Teacher (Amish Country Brides)
The Widower (Amish Country Brides)
The Keeper (Amish Country Brides)
The Pretender (Amish Country Brides)
The Arrangement (featured in the Amish Spring Romance collection)
The Healer (Amish Country Brides)
The Newcomer (Amish Country Brides) The Prequel

UNLIKELY AMISH CHRISTMAS

Unlikely Santa
Unlikely Sweethearts
Unlikely Singing (More Amish Christmas Miracles)
Unlikely Season

FAIRY TALES

The Princess and the Prayer Kapp (Cindy's Story & Rosabelle's Story)

OTHER

Learning to Love –Saul's Story (Sequel to
Chloe's Revelation)
Her Amish Identity
An Unexpected Christmas Gift

COMING 2023 (Lord Willing)

A Forbidden Amish Courtship
A Widower's Amish Courtship

BOOKS by J.E.B. SPREDEMANN

AMISH GIRLS SERIES

Joanna's Struggle

Danika's Journey

Chloe's Revelation

Susanna's Surprise

Annie's Decision

Abigail's Triumph

Brooke's Quest

Leah's Legacy

A Christmas of Mercy –Amish Girls Holiday

Unofficial Glossary
of Pennsylvania Dutch Words

Ach –Oh

Boppli/Bopplin –Baby/Babies

Bruder/Brieder –Brother/Brothers

Chust –Just

Daed/Dat –Dad

Dawdi –Grandfather

Denki –Thanks

Der Herr –The Lord

Dochder(n) –Daughter(s)

Dummkopp –Dummy

Englischer –A non-Amish person

Fraa –Wife/Missus

G'may –Members of an Amish fellowship

Gott –God

Gross sohn –Grandson

Gut –Good

Jah –Yes

Kapp – Amish head covering

Kinner –Children

Maed/Maedel –Girls/Girl

Mamm –Mom

Rumspringa –Running around period for Amish youth

Schatzi –Sweetheart

Schweschder(n) –Sister(s)

Sohn –Son

Wunderbaar – Wonderful

Characters in the
Unlikely Amish Christmas series

Christopher Stoltz a.k.a. "Santa" - Bishop of the local
Amish community (now in the *Bann* for
fellowshipping with his shunned son, James)
(*Unlikely Singing*)

Judy Stoltz - Christopher's faithful wife (*Unlikely
Singing*)

James Stoltz - Christopher and Judy's only living
child, ex-Amish

Robin Stoltz - James' *Englisch* wife

Wesley Stoltz - James and Robin's oldest son
(*Unlikely Santa*)

Shannon Parker Stoltz - Wesley's wife (*Unlikely
Santa*)

Olivia Stoltz - Wesley and Shannon's daughter

Noah Stoltz - Wesley and Shannon's son

Brighton, Jaycee, and Melanie Parker - Shannon's
younger siblings

Randy Stoltz - James and Robin's youngest son
(*Unlikely Sweethearts*)

Holly Remington Stoltz - Randy's Wife (*Unlikely
Sweethearts*)

Trevor - James's *Englisch* friend

AUTHOR'S NOTE

The Amish/Mennonite people and their communities differ one from another. There are, in fact, no two Amish communities exactly alike. It is this premise on which this book is written. I have taken cautious steps to assure the authenticity of Amish practices and customs. Old Order Amish and New Order Amish may be portrayed in this work of fiction and may differ from some communities. Although the book may be set in a certain locality, the practices featured in the book may not necessarily reflect that particular district's beliefs or culture. This book is purely fictional and built around a fictional community, even though you may see similarities to real-life people, practices, and occurrences.

We, as *Englischers*, can learn a lot from the Plain People and their simple way of life. Their hard work, close-knit family life, and concern for others are to be applauded. As the Lord wills, may this special culture continue to be respected and remain so for many centuries to come, and may the light of God's salvation reach their hearts.

ONE

The most wonderful time of the year was upon them again.

James Stoltz examined the naked pine tree awaiting its festive bling in the center of his living room, its heady aroma filling his senses. Before he knew it, his and Robin's quiet home would be bustling with noise and activity.

His son Wesley's crew always brought a bundle of energy—mainly his daughter-in-law's youngest brother, Jaycee. The kid could outpace a circus ringmaster. Fortunately, Wesley was great at handling the boy.

James couldn't help the wave of pride he felt when he thought of his two boys, Wesley and Randy, and the men they had become—although pride had always been looked down upon in his Amish heritage. *Hochmut* was what his people called it.

He snapped out of his musings the moment Robin's

arms slipped around his waist. After salvation, his wife and her family were truly the best thing that had ever happened to him. He did not know where he would be if he hadn't met her.

"Good morning, handsome. Are you ready to have our house turned upside down?"

He chuckled as he turned and indulged his wife with a kiss. He could hardly believe they were nearing thirty years of marriage.

Nearly thirty years of his folks' absence in his life. Thankfully, though, that had all changed a few years ago when God had granted him a miracle and his parents had shown up on his doorstep on Christmas morning.

It was a gift he hoped he'd never take for granted.

Pleasure surged through Christopher Stoltz's entire being as his eyes scanned the glistening path to the barn. He wiped the condensation from a pane on the mudroom window to get a better look. *Der Herr's* wonders never ceased to amaze him. He'd never tire of a snow-covered field or of a sleigh ride with his *fraa*. Although, if he wished to enjoy the latter nowadays, he'd need to hire an *Englisch* driver to take them to his *gross sohn* Wesley's place.

Ach, it had been such a joy to see the *kinskinner's* faces light up last year when he and Judy had gifted them with "Santa's" sleigh, as then-seven-year-old Jaycee had called it. It still tickled Christopher's funny bone when he thought of his now-grandson's innocent mix-up. It wasn't everyday an Amish man was mistaken for Jolly Old Saint Nick.

"What was that chuckle for, *schatzi*?" Judy's voice carried from the kitchen.

The scent of apples and cinnamon drew his attention even more than his *fraa's* words. He turned from the window. "*Chust* remembering when I first met young Jaycee."

A sympathetic smile—the exact one she'd worn three-and-a-half years ago when he'd first told her the story—graced his wife's lips. "Where would we be now if that incident hadn't occurred?"

"In a lot less hot water with the *g'may*, that's for sure." He shook his head as he stepped into the kitchen.

If only they could find a happy medium between the church leaders and their *Englisch sohn's* family. Because they'd broken the rules and chosen to fellowship with James, their only living—ex-Amish— son, the leadership interpreted it as an act of rebellion

3

against the *Ordnung*. That action, along with more Bible study than what the leaders deemed appropriate for their *g'may*, had earned them a shunning.

"*Jah.* But with a lot less joy too. *Der Herr* knew what He was doing when he put you in Jaycee's path. That was no coincidence." Judy had always been *gut* at reminding him what was important.

"*Der Herr* always knows what He's doing. Sometimes it takes us a while to figure it out, though."

"I don't think we need to have all the answers, ain't so? As long as *Gott* knows, that's *gut* enough for me."

"Sometimes I think you would have made a better bishop than me, *fraa*." His absurd comment earned him a laugh.

"Wouldn't the leaders love that comment." She playfully slapped his arm. "Nonsense. You were a *gut* bishop, and everyone knows that. Everyone loved you. And they still do."

His gaze followed his wife longingly as she moved two apple pies from the blazing hot oven to the cooling rack. He sighed, attempting to not think about the predicament they'd gotten themselves into. Life was too short, and they'd already wasted too many years apart from their son and his *kinner*. Having James and his family in their lives was truly a gift from *Gott*.

If they had to endure the shunning for the rest of

their days, then they would—although that wasn't their preference. They both missed fellowshipping with the *g'may*. Their fellow Amish church members had stepped into the role of the family they didn't have for many years, the family they'd lost.

Even Kendal, his best friend since they'd both been scholars in their single-room Amish schoolhouse, had been forced to disfellowship with him. But Christopher knew Kendal understood the rules and was simply following them—something every church member was required to do, whether they agreed or not. The shunning was a painful experience for everyone.

Christopher and Judy detested having to choose between a relationship with their family and a relationship with the church. The funny thing was that for several decades, Christopher had been the one to enforce the shunning of other errant members of the *g'may*. As bishop, it had been one of his duties. Only now, since he'd experienced being on the other side, did he realize how much suffering the *Bann* enacted.

Surely, this was not what *Der Herr* had intended. As Christopher had studied the Scriptures, he'd learned that a true shunning according to the Bible was only to be enacted when one was living in blatant sin and refused to repent. Neither he nor Judy believed their situation applied. If only they could get the other leaders to see.

"I guess I'd better get my chores done if we're to go visit James today." His slice of pie would still be there later, although he yearned for it now. He'd just have to secure a piece before James and the boys decided to get seconds. If Wesley and Randy's families kept growing, Judy would need to start making three or four pies to take along.

"Fortunately, the *Englisch* have no qualms about giving us rides. I'm glad the shunning doesn't stop *them*." A sad smile flashed, then quickly disappeared from Judy's face.

"Even if it did, Randy or Wesley would be happy to give us a ride." He leaned over and kissed his *fraa* on the cheek before donning his boots and hat and slipping out the door.

Shunning or not, today was shaping up to be a lovely day. He'd get to see his family—something he'd gone way too long without.

TWO

Before Wesley Stoltz even had a chance to set foot on the snowy ground, Jaycee had already bolted from the SUV and was halfway to his parents' door.

Beside him, his wife Shannon laughed as she unfastened her seatbelt. "I'd say he's excited about decorating Grandma and Grandpa's Christmas tree."

"I esited too!" Two-and-a-half-year-old Olivia echoed from her car seat in the back, her smile beaming. Their daughter was growing up way too fast.

"Me three!" Melanie proudly held up her three fingers to demonstrate.

Wesley grinned at his young sister-in-law's excitement. It was hard to believe she'd be starting kindergarten next school year. Under Shannon's tutelage, Melanie had already learned her letters and numbers and could read simple words. Wesley didn't know how his wife did it all.

Brighton helped Melanie from her booster. Wesley was amazed at the young man he was becoming. Before they knew it, he'd be bringing home eligible young women. Hopefully, that was still a few years out.

His brother-in-law pointed to the vehicle turning into the driveway. "Uncle Randy and Aunt Holly are here. Do you think he'll want to go ice skating?"

Wesley frowned, then lifted his daughter into his arms and kissed her cheek. "We're here to decorate Grandma and Grandpa's tree. Maybe we'll all go ice skating another day."

"Or we can go snowboarding at Perfect North Slopes." His brother-in-law's face brightened even more.

"I'm not sure Randy will want to go since Holly's so close to birth." Shannon waved to Holly as their pregnant sister-in-law and Wesley's brother Randy walked toward them hand in hand. She unfastened little Noah from his child restraint.

Randy's smile broadened as he eyed his wife of a year and a half. "It looks like we might get a Christmas baby."

Shannon and Wesley shared a look.

"Really? I thought you weren't due until January?" He eyed Holly's abdomen. She was about the size Shannon had been when she'd given birth to their second child.

"I don't know. My mom had most of us early." Holly shrugged. "She seems to think I'll be the same way."

Shannon laughed. "I'm not sure if that's something a person inherits."

Wesley's heart clenched as he thought of his wife. She'd never had the chance to discuss her pregnancies with her own mother. He wondered if she ever dwelled on that fact.

"I guess we'll find out, right?" Holly moved close and side-hugged both Shannon and Wesley.

Randy followed suit but bumped Wesley's shoulder instead of embracing him. It was a guy thing.

"Let me take this sweet one off your hands." Holly reached for Noah and promptly planted a kiss on his ruddy cheek.

Wesley stood amazed as he studied their growing families. Who would have imagined him and his younger brother both married with children before thirty? Of course, he'd gained Brighton, Jaycee, and Melanie right off the bat when he'd taken Shannon as his wife.

He couldn't even imagine the heartbreak they'd all experienced before he met them. At eighteen, Shannon had shown amazing strength in helping her younger siblings deal with their parents' sudden death and keeping their little family together. He fell more in love with her every day.

"What are you thinking about?" Shannon's voice shook him out of his musings.

Wesley glanced around, realizing they were the only two still standing out in his parents' driveway. Randy and Holly must've ushered the little ones inside.

He grinned at his wife and pulled her into his arms. His fingers moved over her beautiful face. "Just thinking about how much I admire my wife," he murmured.

"Oh?" A small smile crept up her lips, anticipating his kiss, no doubt.

He leaned down and oh so gently kissed her cheek. Once. Twice. Moving slowly in the direction of her lips. As much as he enjoyed kissing, leading up to the actual kiss was just as fun. He loved teasing his wife. He'd never tire of hearing that breathless gasp escaping her lips just before his mouth found hers.

"You guys coming in sometime today?" Dad called from the house. "The kids are *dying* to start decorating. Well, at least Jaycee is."

He groaned then reluctantly parted with his wife, laughing. "Give us another minute, will ya?" Moments alone with his wife were few and far between in their busy household. They should be able to enjoy at least a few minutes of quiet, shouldn't they?

Shannon stepped back, but love sparkled in her eyes. "We'd better go in, babe. No telling what's going on in there."

He stared at her longingly but sighed in defeat. "You're right."

She leaned close and whispered, "We can steal away into your old bedroom for a kiss or two later."

His heart rate sped up at the thought. "You can bet I'll claim that promise."

"I'm counting on it." She winked.

He was half tempted to abandon the kids to his parents' care and disappear with his wife for the remainder of the day.

"Come on, my love. We've got a tree to decorate." She intertwined her fingers with his, urging him toward the house.

Just as they reached the door, *Dawdi* and *Mammi* Stoltz's driver pulled up.

Wesley lifted a hand to wave. "I'm going to see if they need help. You know they always bring goodies along." He grinned and encouraged Shannon to continue inside the house. He didn't want her to be out in the cold any longer than he'd already kept her.

"I want to say hello first." Shannon had taken to his Amish grandparents the moment they'd met.

He followed his wife toward his Amish grandparents'

taxi. "Yeah, but Jaycee might—"

"If your mother didn't have them under control, we would have heard about it by now." She laughed, then reached out to hug *Mammi*.

Mom usually had a pretty good handle on things. After all, she and Dad had raised him and Randy.

"You're right. I guess I shouldn't worry." Wesley shrugged, then hugged *Mammi* too.

"There's no worry your *grossmudder's* apple pie won't cure." Grandpa's chipper smile brought a smile to Wesley's own face.

"Santa!" Jaycee charged out the door at full speed and nearly crashed into Grandpa Christopher.

Shannon gasped. "Jaycee!"

"Whoa there, buddy! Let's not put *Grossdawdi* Christopher into an early grave." Wesley grimaced. Perhaps his mother *didn't* have the children under control.

His grandfather swatted the air. "I'm used to Jaycee's enthusiasm. It'll take more than a rambunctious *bu* to put me in my grave."

"He should be more careful, though," Wesley insisted.

He thought Jaycee would have outgrown his fascination with Grandpa Christopher or "Santa" by now. He did know the truth about the fictional character but continued to address Grandpa Christopher as such. He guessed as long as Grandpa didn't mind, it didn't matter. He got the feeling Grandpa Stoltz secretly enjoyed the boy's nickname for him.

"*Be careful for nothing* is what the Good Book says. Our time is in *Der Herr's* hands. He is the one who decides the number of our days. Sometimes I think the *Englischers* give too much heed to the temporary."

Wesley understood trusting God, and he admired the Amish for their stance. However, he *did* think the Amish community sometimes tended to place too little importance on protecting their little ones.

He'd just read of yet another tragedy that had befallen a small boy when he'd been helping his father in his shop. Yes, accidents happened and would continue to. But the senseless death of this young boy could have been prevented. He couldn't imagine living with that kind of guilt and regret.

And of course, there was the other extreme. Keeping your loved ones in a protective bubble wasn't the answer either.

"We must trust *Gott* with everything, *gross sohn.* There is only so much we can control. We must not question what *Der Herr* allows. He knows best. Always."

"I know He does, Grandpa. Thanks for the reminder."

They all finally made their way inside Mom and Dad's house.

Wesley still marveled at the fact that Grandpa and

Grandma Stoltz were even here at his father's house. To tell the truth, he was proud of his grandparents for going against rules that didn't make sense. Just because Dad attended a non-Amish church didn't mean he was a heathen. It just meant that he was serving God according to his own convictions and not those of the Amish church.

"Now that everyone is here, let's say a prayer that God will bless our time together," Dad reached his hand to Mom, who reached for Grandma Judy's hand. Each member of their family created a chain of unity and love as Dad led off their time together with a blessing.

As Dad prayed, Wesley gave thanks for the many gifts God had bestowed upon him and couldn't wait to see what might lie up ahead for all of them.

THREE

Now that the tree was decorated and everyone had eaten a satisfying meal, the adults lounged around the living room enjoying the fire in the hearth. Brighton and Jaycee enjoyed a snowball fight outside and the three youngest ones napped.

With the twinkling lights on the tree, James thought the cozy scene felt like it was straight out of a Christmas movie. Truly, he was a blessed man. He never thought he'd be celebrating the holidays with his folks as long as he remained *Englisch* and they, Amish.

"I always wondered about how the Amish celebrated Christmas. Because Randy said you didn't believe in having a tree, right?" His most recent daughter-in-law, Holly, leaned against the couch and rubbed her rounded belly. Another blessing their family would enjoy resided within her womb. As long as all went well with her labor and delivery, they'd be holding their third grandchild in their arms soon.

Randy had expressed his concern for his wife on more than one occasion, and James speculated by the furrow on his son's brow that he worried now. He'd known about Holly's health issues prior to marrying her, but James wondered if his son had considered the implications her condition would have on childbearing.

James and Robin had encouraged their son to place his wife and baby in the Lord's hands. He was the healer and the giver of life, and He alone knew what the future held for them. Randy had never been strong in his faith, but meeting Holly certainly encouraged him in that department. No doubt, these current trials were building his faith, and for that they were thankful.

"I reckon it's not too much different from how the *Englisch* celebrate it. We enjoy food and gifts as well. We just forgo the lights and decorations and fancy trappings and whatnot. We focus on what the season is about—*Gott* sending His Son to the earth," Dad explained.

"I like that." Holly smiled, her gaze focused on the tree. "But I think I'd miss it. The lights. The ornaments."

"Can't miss what you never had," Dad reasoned.

"You're right." Holly nodded. "What about you, James? When did you experience your first non-Amish Christmas? Did you think it was weird?"

"Weird?" His brow lowered. "Not really. I had *Englisch* friends, so I was aware of the different traditions."

"How old were you?" She tilted her head to the right and her lips bent upward. "You know, I never heard the story about how you and Robin met."

"We've never heard it either." Mom sat up straighter, then glanced at Dad. "We'd like to hear it too. *Ain't so*, Christopher?"

Dad frowned, then agreed with Mom and nodded.

"Are you sure?" James studied his folks, then glanced at Robin to make sure his wife was comfortable with the conversation. He raised an eyebrow and she nodded. "You're sure?"

"You guys are acting pretty mysterious about all this." Randy rubbed his wife's shoulders.

"Well, it would have to start way back before I met your mom. When I was Amish." James eyed his parents. "Are you comfortable with me telling the kids about the past?"

"I have nothing to hide. We've all made plenty of mistakes, that is for sure." A sad smile appeared on Dad's face.

James knew his parents carried many regrets, as did he. He took a deep breath, then he allowed his mind to wander back to a time when he was much much younger...

FOUR

James had a feeling something was going on when *Dat* dropped him off at his friend Leo's house. *Mamm* was sick—that was what he'd guessed—although she'd tried not to act like it.

His first clue was when *Dat* made breakfast. *Dat* never made breakfast.

As a matter of fact, *Mamm* hardly let *Dat* set foot into the kitchen while she was fixing meals. Of course, James couldn't blame *Mamm* for that. *Dat* always got underfoot and tried to sample everything before it made its way to the table. One time, he'd distracted *Mamm* and the rolls she'd put into the cookstove turned black.

Mamm hadn't been happy about that at all.

James had waited patiently for *Dat* to come and get him. It had been his first and only time staying the night at someone's house, and he didn't much care for it.

He'd missed *Mamm* and *Dat* too much.

What made matters worse was that Leo's folks acted like they knew something neither he nor Leo knew. "When you get home, there will be a surprise waiting for you," Leo's *mamm* had said.

It was all rather confusing. That was, until he stepped into his home the next day.

The last thing he imagined his surprise would be was a *boppli*. A baby *bruder*, to be specific. But there he was. Kendal Stoltz, all pink and crying.

With five years between them, James knew he had to be the one to watch out for his baby brother. And he was happy to do it until his *bruder* turned one-and-a-half. Kendal couldn't hardly stay out of mischief!

"He's *chust* curious," *Dat* would say.

"*Jah*, but I'm curious too and I never eat bugs."

Dat simply laughed.

Other than Kendal getting into mischief, he was a fun sibling to be around. He could talk a body's ear off. James preferred reading or working quietly and tried to mind his own business. Kendal didn't know what it meant to mind one's own business, it seemed. *Nee*, he wanted to know what everyone was doing all the time.

Three years later, baby Katie came along. If there ever was a *boppli* that was doted over, it was little

Katie, for sure. She was the sweetest little thing and always happy. They were all happy.

But that happiness had been short lived.

FIVE

*K*endal had been six, Katie just three.

None of them could have foreseen the events that would take place that beautiful spring day. It was the first time James had truly thought about death. It's interesting how one moment a person could be living a carefree life with not a trouble in the world, and then BAM! Your entire world is turned upside down.

Like when that *Englischer's* truck slammed into the side of their buggy.

James remembered the accident in vivid detail. He'd been holding the reins and *Mamm* had been in the passenger's seat closest to the traffic. Kendal and Katie had been sitting in back.

Even though *Mamm* and *Dat* had assured him many times that it hadn't been his fault, James had always felt like he was partially responsible for the accident. What if he'd turned onto the shoulder to allow the cars to pass? If he'd veered slightly right, would Kendal and Katie still be here today?

Why had his life been spared when his younger siblings hadn't been? Why had *Mamm* sustained life-changing injuries and he pretty much remained unscathed?

These were questions he'd asked himself many times, but there never seemed to be an answer.

"It was *Gott's* will," *Dat* had insisted. "*Der Herr* gives life and He takes away. It is His business alone."

The funeral had been the worst day of his life. Aside from the two well-deserved spankings he'd earned growing up, he'd never cried in his life. Well, maybe he had as a *boppli*. But he'd cried many tears that day— more than he knew he possessed. He'd never see his little *bruder* and *schweschder* again, and that fact had injured his heart.

After the accident, his whole life changed. And yet it stayed the same. He continued with school—alone— until he'd finished at fourteen. Then he worked with *Dat* on his small construction crew.

Neither *Mamm* nor *Dat* talked about Kendal and Katie much after that. James hadn't been sure why. Maybe it was too painful, or they didn't want him to heap more guilt upon himself. Either way, it made James sad. He didn't want to continue on with life as though his younger brother and sister never existed. He wanted to remember their happy times together, although some days with Kendal *had* been trying, he admitted to himself.

Mamm's smile had never been the same since that fateful day.

James knew, at seventeen, he'd decide to get baptized in the Amish church. After all, that was the way of things in his culture and what was expected of him. Besides, he had no plans to leave *Mamm* and *Dat*.

It wasn't until he turned eighteen that he met his *Englisch* friend, Trevor. Both Trevor and his brother taxied for the Amish, and they sometimes shared construction jobs. Their father had been an electrician, so working together had happened often in the two years they'd known each other.

James liked Trevor right away and sensed in his soul that something was different about him. Occasionally, he and Trevor found themselves driving to the hardware store alone. It was then that James had taken the opportunities to ask his friend about *Englisch* things that had been foreign to him.

JENNIFER SPREDEMANN

Besides being educated in common *Englisch* things like listening to the radio—something that wasn't allowed in his community—and seeing a movie or two, James learned about Trevor's family.

They, too, had lost loved ones. But when Trevor had spoken of them, there was hope behind his words. He spoke as though dying was a blessing and he couldn't wait until he entered Heaven. His words had been confusing and intriguing at the same time.

"Hey, James. Why don't you come to church with me one of these days?" Trevor's smile stretched across his face like it always did.

He should have said, "No, thank you." Instead, he asked, "When?"

"You already go to church on Sunday mornings, right?"

"Just every other Sunday, but on off-Sundays we usually visit with other members in the community."

"How about Sunday night, then?"

James grimaced. Sunday night was when he met with the other *youngie* in his community for singing and such. Besides, he was supposed to take Susan Schwartz home in his buggy on Sunday. "I don't think that would work."

"Or maybe our midweek Bible study and prayer service?"

"I don't know, Trevor. Could my folks come along too?"

"Yeah, sure. Do you think they would? Isn't your father a minister or something?"

"You're right. They wouldn't go." James frowned, although the thought of going intrigued him. If nothing else, he wanted to go just to see what it was like.

"We also have a youth event coming up. Why don't you come with me? You could meet new people. I think you would like it."

"When is it?"

"Friday night."

James scratched his head. "Can I let you know tomorrow?"

James could think of little else for the remainder of the week. *Dat* wouldn't like him going with Trevor. He already knew that.

Unlike some other worldly Amish districts, their community didn't allow for a *rumspringa*. He hadn't even known what it was until Trevor had explained it. The thought of Amish parents encouraging and permitting their young folks to indulge in a worldly lifestyle just seemed wrong, to James's thinking.

James didn't have any desire to live worldly, per se, but he would like to try some things that weren't allowed in his community. Like seeing how the

Englischers' church was. How different was it from his own community? Did they sing the same songs and listen to preaching and have kneeling prayer?

By the time he saw Trevor again, he'd made up his mind. He would go with his friend. After all, what harm could there be in learning how other folks worshipped *Gott*?

SIX

This youth meeting had been quite a bit different than any that James had gone to in his Amish community. Some aspects had been similar, though. Eating with other young folks and singing hadn't been all that different, although the singing at Trevor's youth meeting was accompanied by an acoustic guitar and they lounged around on couches and chairs instead of sitting across from each other at a long table.

James had thought it rather enjoyable. What would *Dat* say if James decided to take up playing a musical instrument like the guitar? The only thing he'd heard played in his community was a mouth harp. He'd never asked, but he was quite certain other instruments would be *verboten*.

"You should give it a try," Trevor encouraged. "I could teach you."

"Really?"

"Sure. You can even borrow my extra steel string at home. I hardly play that one anymore."

"I couldn't take it home."

A look of regret flashed across Trevor's face. "Oh, I forgot, man. It's not allowed, is it?"

"Well, I never really asked but I'm thinking no." James frowned.

"You could come over to my house and we can jam together." He handed James one of the guitars someone had been playing earlier. The other young folks seemed to be mingling, talking, laughing, discussing. The atmosphere was quite inviting.

James took the guitar offered to him. "You're sure this is okay?"

Trevor laughed. He had the other guitar that had been used while they'd been singing. "We're good. Now slip that strap over your shoulder so it goes behind your back."

James did as told.

"Now watch my fingers and do as I do, okay?" Trevor held some strings down with several of his fingers, then strummed the other end with what he'd called a pick.

James attempted to do the same thing, but it sounded off.

"I think you missed a string." Trevor helped him position his fingers. "Now try it."

He couldn't help but smile when the tune actually came out right.

"See. You've got it. That was the G chord. If you learn just a few more—A, C, and D—and you learn to transition well, you'll have the foundation to play many songs."

"Really?" His excitement surged.

"Here. Just watch this." Trevor began playing. "Keep an eye on my fingers."

James's gaze stayed riveted on Trevor's movements as a familiar tune emerged from the strings.

Trevor finished his line. "Did you recognize that? It was 'Silent Night.'"

"You only used three chords the whole time?"

"Good eye." He nodded. "Now, you *can* play it a lot fancier, but you don't have to."

"Could you teach me that?" James grinned. *Ach*, it would be *wunderbaar* to know how to play a musical instrument.

"Sure. But we'll have to get together another time and practice because I think we're about to head out."

James's excitement deflated. "Oh, is it over already?" He'd been having such a *gut* time.

"Nah. We're planning to go on a scavenger hunt."

He frowned. "How do you do that?"

"Don't worry, the leaders will explain exactly what we're supposed to do." Trevor pointed to the main guy who'd led the singing and Bible study, who encouraged everyone to gather around.

"Okay, who all's got a car?" The main guy asked.

Many of the young folks lifted a hand, including Trevor.

The man looked at a few different people. "Did you bring your cameras?"

Several of the young people held up cameras. James had seen this kind before—they were the neat ones that produced an instant photo.

"Okay. We're going to divide up into four teams. Five people on each team. Trevor, your guest can go with you. Everyone else, line up." The man began going through the group assigning each person a one, two, three, or four. "Drivers, you will be the team leaders."

Every team received a piece of paper with a list of items on it. "There are six tasks on each of your lists. You must complete each task and be back here no later than nine thirty. That gives you two hours. You must take a photo as you complete each task, and *every* team member needs to be present in the photo."

Trevor leaned over to James. "Are you okay with that?"

James shrugged. "It's part of the game, right?"

Trevor nodded, so James agreed.

"Remember," The youth leader continued. "You must leave a Gospel tract with at least one person at every stop." He paused. "Is everybody ready?"

The group cheered with enthusiasm.

"We'll pray, then you all can head out." They all bowed their heads then the leader said a prayer asking for safety and that God would use the Gospel tracts and people would get saved. As soon as he finished the prayer, each team scrambled for the vehicles and set off on their adventures.

The exciting evening continued. James, Trevor, and the other three in their group—another guy and two girls—checked off each item. They'd gone to the airport and taken a photo with one of the workers there. They found a police officer, explained what they were doing, then had the officer handcuff one of them for the photo. They'd gone to a nearby park and taken a picture of their group on the playground equipment, and the list went on.

Every group managed to complete their tasks and arrive back at the leader's house safely. It had been fun hearing all the stories and seeing the photos from each group's adventure.

Trevor dropped him back off at home with a promise

to pick him up tomorrow. They had plans to practice guitar. James couldn't wait to learn a song or two.

He couldn't remember the last time he'd been this excited about life. Had he *ever* been this excited about life?

But that excitement quickly deflated the moment he stepped into his house that night.

Dat sat in his chair, a frown on his face.

Ach, he hadn't expected *Dat* to still be up at this hour. "*Vas is lets?*"

"I think you know what is wrong, *sohn*." *Dat's* scowl deepened. "Had a visit from the deacon an hour ago. You were seen posing for a photograph with some *Englischers*."

James's brow lowered. "*Jah*. I was with Trevor's church group."

"When you were baptized, you became a member of the *g'may*. You are not allowed to spend time with Trevor's church group."

"But why? We weren't doing anything bad."

"You are Amish, not *Englisch*. You must remember that."

Ire rose in his chest. "But you have *Englisch* friends."

"Do you see me going to their churches?"

"No, but—"

"I visit with them when they stop by because to do

otherwise would be rude. We help those in need. But our fellowship must be among the *g'may*, not with the *Englisch*." *Dat* stood, as though their conversation was over. "Best you find a *maedel* and settled down, *ain't so*?"

"You want me to cut ties with Trevor?" His heart sank.

"That would probably be best." *Dat* squeezed his arm, then disappeared into his and *Mamm's* bedroom.

James stood alone in the quiet living room, attempting to process all that had just taken place. Moisture gathered in his eyes unbidden. He'd just experienced one of the most amazing days of his life and now he had to give it all up?

What about his guitar lessons with Trevor? What about his agreement to return to the youth group next week? What about the new friends he'd made?

Just when life was beginning to look up, his world had come crashing down. Again.

SEVEN

"What happened?" Trevor took James aside the following week at the construction site when *Dat* had been busy discussing blueprints with the homeowner.

"One of the church leaders saw me out with your youth group. I'm forbidden to go again." James grimaced.

"Is that why you stood me up for our guitar lessons? I thought you wanted to learn."

"I did. I do. But I can't." Sorrow filled his heart at the finality of his words.

"Why not?"

"It's against the rules."

"I thought you guys followed the Bible. Haven't you read Psalm 150?"

"I don't know." James shrugged. "Probably."

"Well, then?"

"What?"

"Read it. Then we'll talk."

"I'll have to see if I can get ahold of *Dat's* Bible, then."

Trevor's jaw slacked. "You don't have your own Bible?"

"I'll have one when I set up my own house. Every Amish family owns a *Heilige Schrift*."

"A what?"

"A German Bible."

"You read German? I thought you spoke Pennsylvania Dutch or something."

"I learned some German in school."

"So, you can speak Pennsylvania Dutch and German and English? And you only went to school through the eighth grade? Wow. That's impressive."

"I can read and understand a little German. By no means is it my strong point."

"But your Bible is in German?" Trevor scratched his head. "That's a little confusing."

"It's just the way our people have always done things. We try to keep the old ways."

"So, do you actually understand the Bible when you read it?"

James frowned. "I don't...*Dat* reads it, then he explains what he read to us."

"It sounds like we need to have guitar lessons *and* Bible study." Trevor gave him that look—the look that said, "You know I'm right."

"I already told you that I'm not allowed to."

"Fine. But I'm getting you an English Bible that you can read and *understand*. You're allowed to have an English Bible, right?"

Ach. Englischers just didn't get their ways. What was James thinking? *He* didn't even understand the ways of his people. Why *did* they read a German Bible and not a translation they could better understand?

Maybe he'd talk to *Dat* tonight and ask him questions about the thoughts he'd been having.

James had resigned himself to the Amish ways, but Trevor's words kept coming back. What had he meant when he mentioned Psalm 150?

"*Dat*, what does Psalm 150 say?" James approached his father as he relaxed in his chair after supper.

Dat's brow lowered and he reached for his Bible. He proceeded to read the chapter Trevor had mentioned.

James thought he understood most of it. It had been about praising *Der Herr*. The verse that stuck out to him, though, was about praising *Gott* with stringed instruments. That would include a guitar, to his thinking.

"Why don't our people use instruments like guitars?"

"They are of the world, *sohn*."

"But the harmonica is not?" This didn't make sense, to James's thinking.

"*Nee*. Our people have used a mouth harp for a long time."

"But we just read about praising *Gott* with stringed instruments. Wouldn't that include the guitar?"

Dat's brow furrowed. "I don't know, *sohn*."

"Why do we only read from the German Bible and not an *Englisch* one?" It hadn't been James's intention to challenge the Amish ways, but he needed real answers.

"It's the pure language."

"What does that mean?"

"*Gott* helped Martin Luther translate it into German."

"But what about the *Englisch* Bible? Didn't *Gott* help translate that too? Trevor read a verse from his Bible. I think it was a King James Bible. The words were about men being moved by the Holy Ghost. He said it is a *gut* translation. He said it's the same as Martin Luther's Bible, but in English."

His father sighed and James sensed his growing discomfort. "I don't know about all that, *sohn*. I've never studied about the *Englisch* Bibles. I only know the German Bible is a *gut* one."

"But what if I don't understand it? My German isn't that *gut*. How will I teach my family what it says if I can't understand it myself?"

"Perhaps you need to return to your German studies, then."

"Or get an English Bible." His body warmed the moment the words left his lips. Goodness, he'd never spoken to *Dat* so frankly.

Dat stared at him and for a long moment he thought *Dat* might say something he'd regret. "What is all this worldly talk? I think you have been spending too much time with *Englischers*. Best you cut ties with Trevor."

Cut ties with Trevor? Altogether?

He wanted to protest. He wanted to ask what was worldly about wanting to read and understand the Bible and praise *Der Herr* with instruments. But he wouldn't. He knew when *Dat* was at his limit and James had hit it. Any more discussion would not end well for either of them. It was better to just keep his thoughts to himself.

But he'd already determined one thing. If Trevor brought him an English Bible, James wouldn't refuse it.

EIGHT

James was dying to talk to Trevor.

Where had his friend been lately? James hadn't seen him since they'd met secretly a week ago and he'd been gifted his English Bible.

He desperately wanted to discuss what he'd been reading in his Bible with Trevor. He wished he could talk to *Dat* about these things, but he knew it would only lead to strife. James wanted to avoid strife as much as possible.

Especially since their bishop's recent passing. *Dat* already had enough on his plate. His name would go into the lot for their district's next leader at the next communion service, which was quickly approaching. James prayed *Dat's* name wouldn't be chosen.

James wasn't even sure if he would take communion this time. If the *g'may* frowned upon reading an English Bible, he'd be expected to confess his "sin" and renounce it. He had no plans to do so. Especially when he knew deep in his soul there wasn't anything wrong with reading the Bible in English. Wouldn't confessing a sin that wasn't really a sin be like lying to *Der Herr*?

He'd just read about Ananias and Sapphira. They'd lied to the church leaders and dropped dead just like that. In this case, James feared *Gott* more than man. He refused to confess a sin that didn't exist.

James was beginning to wonder if *Dat* had told Trevor not to come around anymore. Either that, or his friend had taken ill. He hadn't shown up at the job site they'd both been working at, which raised concern.

Perhaps he should hire a driver to take him to Trevor's house. He needed to make sure his friend was all right. He'd thought of calling until he realized someone had access to all the numbers that were dialed out from the phone shanty. There was no such thing as a secret phone call in his community.

Besides, he wanted to see Trevor face to face. He missed his friend's presence in his life. Trevor had been closer than any ties he'd made in the Amish community. James had friends, but no one he could really talk to like Trevor. He valued a friend he could be open and honest with. He felt like he could share anything with his *Englisch* friend without judgement or worry that he'd be reported to the deacon.

That was one of the things about the *g'may* that had bothered him. Some folks felt it was their duty to report infractions to the leaders—like the person who'd seen him posing for a photograph.

James had barely raised his fist to knock on the door when Trevor pulled it open.

His friend glanced behind him. "Does your dad know you're here?"

"*Nee*. He wouldn't approve."

"Yeah, I know. He had a few choice words with me. Told me to stay away from you." Trevor shook his head and sighed. "I really don't get all your Amish rules, man."

"I know. I don't either, honestly." He followed Trevor to his room. A large suitcase sat open on his friend's bed. "What's this all about? Are you going somewhere?"

"Yeah. Did you hear about the recent storms they had down in the Oklahoma-Arkansas area?"

"Tornadoes, right?"

Trevor nodded. "There was a lot of damage. Some of us from the church are going down there to help out. Rebuild houses and all that."

Compassion surged in James's gut. "I know how to do all that. I could help."

Trevor's expression widened. "Do you think your church would let you go?"

"I don't see why not. We help out here when there are storms and such." Excitement began building in his chest. "When do you leave?"

"Two days. Would you really come?"

"I want to."

"That would be great. We can use as many hands as possible and I'm not sure how many of the guys actually have any construction experience. You'd be a welcome addition to our team."

"I'll tell *Dat* about it tonight. I'm sure he'll be fine with me going."

"Do you think so?" Trevor cast a doubtful gaze.

"Why would *Der Herr* put this perfect opportunity in my path and give me the skills needed to help these people if He didn't want me to go?"

Trevor raised his hands. "Good question."

"I have a lot more questions." James grinned. "I've been reading my English Bible."

"That's great. Do you understand it?"

"Way better than *Dat's* German Bible, that's for sure."

"Well, ask away." Trevor smiled.

NINE

James had a difficult time controlling his excitement when he bounded through the door at suppertime. It looked like his timing was perfect.

"What has you so excited?" *Mamm's* smile filled her face, but *Dat's* demeanor told a different story.

"I wanted to talk to you guys about something." He looked back and forth from *Mamm* to *Dat*.

"Let us eat." *Dat* gestured for him to sit down. "The talking can wait until after supper."

Was it just James's imagination or had this been the slowest meal they'd ever eaten? *Dat* seemed to take his sweet time and made sure to get seconds. James could hardly eat a thing. By the time *Dat finally* said the prayer signaling the meal's end, James thought he might burst.

Then he had to wait until everything was put away and the dishes were done. He'd volunteered to do them, but *Mamm* refused his help.

Ach, could this evening proceed even slower? With his luck, someone would show up at the door and keep *Mamm* and *Dat* occupied until it was time to retire for bed.

The seconds ticked by as James tapped his pant leg.

The moment *Mamm* joined them in the living room, James began his exposition. "You know there were storms down in Oklahoma and Arkansas last week, right?"

His folks both nodded, their eyes trained on him.

"Well, I want to go down there and help with cleanup and reconstruction. Is that okay with you?" His gaze ping-ponged from *Dat* to *Mamm*, gauging their reactions.

"Who is going?" *Dat's* brow lowered.

"Well, Trevor's church—"

"Trevor?"

"*Jah*. I—"

"I thought I told you to cut ties with that *Englischer*." *Dat* did not look happy with him. This wasn't *gut*.

"*Jah*, you did but I was worried about him since he hadn't shown up at our jobsite."

"I fired him. Him and his *bruder* won't be working with our crew any longer."

Dat's words felt like a slap across the face. Might as well have been.

48

Ire burned like a fire in his chest. "How could you fire him, *Dat*? He's a *gut* worker and my friend."

"You do not need *Englisch* friends. There are plenty of folks here in our community to form friendships with. He is not a *gut* influence on you. As long as he's been around, you've be dreaming about the *Englisch* world. We can't have that."

James's heart ached. "Does that mean that you don't want me to go help out?"

"What do you think?" *Dat's* frown deepened.

"I think *Der Herr* wants me to go on this trip and help out people who need the skills *Gott* has given me." He knew opposing *Dat* could carry consequences, but if he didn't follow his conscience, what kind of a man would he be?

"You will use the skills *I* taught you to live among the *Englisch*?" James heard the offense in *Dat's* tone.

"Not live among them. I just plan to go help out." He attempted to remain calm, although he was feeling anything but.

"That's how it begins." *Dat's* stare pierced right through his heart. "If you think *Der Herr* would have you do something that is against the *Ordnung* and will cause you to deliberately disobey your *vatter*, you are mistaken, *sohn*."

"With all due respect, *Dat*, I don't think I am mistaken."

Dat sneered. "Respect? Respect is obeying your folks."

"Why would *Gott* put this inside me so strong if He didn't want me to do it?" He opened his hands, attempting to reason with him.

"The devil comes as an angel of light. You are being deceived."

"I disagree."

"If you are going to be bullheaded about this, I cannot stop you." *Dat* sighed heavily. "But know *this*. If you leave, you will not be welcome on this property again until you are ready to confess your sins and make peace with the *g'may*." *Dat's* face appeared so hardened it could have been chiseled in stone.

His heart ached at *Dat's* words. "So, you're kicking me out? *Dat*, I just want to go help." Did his voice just squeak? *Ach*, he couldn't believe he was standing up to his *vatter* like this. But everything inside him told him he was doing the right thing.

"The choice is yours."

"I've already made my choice. I'm planning to go. I just hoped you would support me in this." Tears burned his eyes. James pivoted on his heel and headed to his room. He needed to pack his bags if their crew was leaving in two days.

"*Nee!*" *Mamm* cried. "Christopher, *nee*. Stop him."

"I will not stop him. He has made his choice."

James truly felt bad for *Mamm*, but he needed to do what *Der Herr* had laid on his heart. He knew that if he followed *Gott's* will, He would work everything out. Although he hated the fact that *Dat* had taken this as an offense.

TEN

James attempted to get comfortable in the van that was transporting their church crew to the Oklahoma-Arkansas border. But no matter how he positioned his pillow, he just couldn't sleep.

"Troubles?" Trevor had awakened from his short snooze.

"I can't sleep."

"Too excited?"

"Something like that." James released a heavy sigh. "I'll no longer have a home to return to when we get back."

"What?" Trevor's head snapped backward.

"My *dat* said that if I left, I wouldn't be allowed back on their property unless I make a kneeling confession of my sin before the church."

"Seriously?"

James nodded.

"So, you're officially an *Englischer*?"

James shrugged. "I reckon."

Trevor shook his head. "I thought stuff like that only happened in third world countries." He frowned. "I'm sorry, man."

"I still can't believe *Dat* fired you and your *bruder*."

"My brother, you mean?" Trevor teased. "You better lose your Amish if you're going to be an *Englischer* from now on."

"*Jah*. You're right."

"It was just a joke. Speak however you want to. You shouldn't care what anyone thinks."

"How much longer do we have?" He peered out at the darkness. They'd switched drivers a couple of hours ago so they could drive well into the night and arrive sooner.

"I'm not sure." Trevor called to the driver. "What time are we scheduled to arrive?"

"Should be at the hotel in a couple more hours. It'll give us all a few hours to sleep before we grab a bite to eat then get to work."

A few hours weren't much, but right now they sounded heavenly, to James's thinking.

Right now, James just wished for a decent bed to lie down on. Last night on Trevor's couch hadn't been comfortable at all. He hadn't been able to bear staying at home a moment longer than necessary. After his altercation with *Dat*, he'd packed his bags and headed for his friend's house the next morning.

He had no idea what he'd do when he returned to Indiana. But, right now, all that mattered was that he complete the task that he knew *Der Herr* had laid on his heart. He was sure *Gott* would work it out.

James was glad when they finally arrived at the hotel.

"Time to get rested up. In the morning, we'll grab a bite to eat from the continental breakfast. We'll leave at eight o'clock sharp. If you're not at the van at that time, you will have to find your own ride to the base church where we will receive our instructions tomorrow morning." The team leader called out to their group. "I believe everyone has their room assignments. Does anyone have any questions?"

Trevor and James shook their heads, along with the rest of the group.

"Okay. I'll be in room 204 if you need to get a hold of me for any reason. Goodnight, everyone. And don't forget to say your prayers."

Everyone chuckled, then parted to their rooms.

It looked like tomorrow would be a busy day. James couldn't help but wonder how *Mamm* and *Dat* were faring without him.

ELEVEN

I t didn't matter where he was or how much sleep he'd had, James woke up at five o'clock sharp Indiana time. Which meant it was only four o'clock here in Arkansas.

He glanced over at the bed next to his in the hotel room. At least Trevor slept soundly.

Continental breakfast wouldn't start until seven o'clock. He sighed, changed positions, then attempted to fall back asleep. It didn't work. He might as well get up and do something constructive.

James didn't want to disturb Trevor, so he took the small coffee maker into the bathroom and closed the door. He examined it momentarily, trying to figure out how to make the thing produce a cup of coffee. He'd never made his own coffee in his life, and this looked quite a bit different than the stainless-steel kettle *Mamm* used on the cookstove at home.

Perhaps there had been instructions on the tray in the other room. He opened the bathroom door and discovered a paper card showing what to do with the thing. He followed the directions and smiled in delight a couple minutes later when he finally held a steaming cup of coffee in his hands.

He thought about the *Englisch* world he'd now be living in. There were so many things he didn't know how to do. Like driving a car. That was a necessity for an *Englischer*. He didn't doubt that Trevor would be willing to teach him.

The *gut* thing about staying over at Trevor's was that he'd learned a little more guitar and had actually been able to practice more than a few minutes like previous times. He was beginning to get the hang of it. He enjoyed playing an instrument, although the tips of his fingers—which now sported blisters—disagreed with him. Trevor assured him they'd turn into callouses in no time.

Since it would be a couple hours before the others awakened, James might as well go and explore the hotel. He thought he'd seen a swimming pool and a gym. Maybe he'd find something to occupy himself until it was time for breakfast.

James had been good and ready to start work when everyone else finally emerged from their hotel rooms. Fortunately, the leader had said the bus ride over to the church wouldn't take long.

"Are you excited?" Trevor gulped down the last of his juice.

"I'm aching to see what we're up against and get started on our projects." James rubbed his hands together. He'd always taken pleasure when working with his hands. The feeling of accomplishment wasn't just a reward for him, it was a need. He had a hard time keeping still—activity had been essential.

Now that he thought about it, he wondered if it had anything to do with the loss of his younger *bruder* and *schweschder*. Keeping busy had been a way to take his mind off hard things that weighed on his mind. Like missing *Mamm* and *Dat* and knowing he wouldn't have a home to return to.

"We're going to have plenty of things to do. They said that the locals had already started cleaning up the areas but there's still a ton of things that need done. It's amazing that something can be demolished within minutes but takes weeks and months to be rebuilt."

That was one thing he liked about living in the Amish community. Everyone came together and things were repaired and rebuilt quickly. And because they were organized and experienced, it wasn't uncommon to have a new barn up within a few days of it being destroyed by a fire or storm.

James wondered if there were any Amish communities close to where these recent storms had hit. If so, they would be a great asset in rebuilding these tornado-ravaged communities.

When they arrived at the base church, the first thing James noticed was that everyone there wore matching T-shirts. Their group was instructed to find a T-shirt from one of the boxes so they could be identified with their church. Everyone was also instructed to write their name on a name tag and introduce themselves.

James felt a little odd wearing the *Englisch* clothing. Although he'd spent time with Trevor, he'd never felt the need to dress *Englisch*.

After a brief prayer for safety, and God's blessing and leading, the entire group loaded up in the church bus and headed to an area that had been ravaged by the prior month's tornado that had blown through the area.

Once they arrived, their large group split up into smaller work crews. The group James was in consisted of four men and two women.

It looked like a lot of cleanup had been done, evidenced by the large piles of debris, but there was still much to be done before they could begin working on the house. This particular area had seen its share of flood water as well, so some of the remaining material was unusable for rebuilding.

They'd been advised to don gloves and masks to prevent contamination and the inhalation of toxic chemicals and debris. Safety seemed to be a top priority and for good reason. These people had already experienced quite a bit of misfortune. No sense in causing more heartache when injuries could be easily prevented with simple safety measures.

TWELVE

As lunchtime rolled around, a crew from the church had come and set up tables with sandwiches, chips, a fruit and vegetable tray, and bottled water.

Although the fall weather was pleasant, the workers' clothes had dampened with perspiration. James would need a shower once they returned to their hotel room.

When James and Trevor made their way to the table for fortification, an attractive *maedel*—young woman—caught James's eye. He couldn't help but smile at the pretty brunette tending the table.

"Thank you for bringing us food." He nodded, glancing to see if she wore a name tag.

"No, thank you for coming to help." She returned his smile, then gestured to his hair. "Are you…Amish?"

Ach. He didn't think he'd be recognized since his suspenders were under the project T-shirt, but the shirt didn't hide his hair. Or his accent. "*Jah.*"

Full plate in hand, he moved to the side so he wouldn't be standing in others' way.

Trevor stepped beside him and squeezed his shoulder. "You mean you *were* Amish."

Did one stop being Amish because they no longer lived in the community? Somehow, he felt that no matter where his life ventured from this point, he'd always be Amish.

"Right. What Trevor said, I guess." He grimaced.

Her brow lowered and she studied him. "But you…I think I'm missing something."

Trevor glanced at James. "Can I tell her or would you rather?"

She shook her head. "He doesn't have to tell me anything. Especially if it's personal."

Admiration filled his heart for this young woman. He suddenly felt like he wanted to tell her everything.

She reached her hand toward him. "I'm Robin Mills."

He nodded and shook her hand. "James Stoltz."

"And I'm Trevor." He shook her hand too.

"Are you going to eat too?" James held up his plate.

"Oh, no, I already had something." She pointed to his plate. "Let me know if you like the cookies. I made them." She winked.

He knew she was just teasing, but why had her gesture caused his heart to flip-flop?

He reached for his cookie and took a bite. He wasn't sure if the cookie was delicious because of the buttery sweetness or because he was eating it in her presence, but he was sure and certain this had to be the best cookie he'd ever eaten.

"*Ach*, it's amazing."

Her grin lit up her entire face. "Aren't they the best? I love them too. Take however many you want. I made several dozen."

He popped the rest of the cookie into his mouth. "*Denk*—thank you. I think I will take a couple more."

"I can put some in a plastic bag for you, if you'd like to take some back to the hotel with you. I'm sure they aren't going to get eaten. I made way too many. I expected there to be more people."

"That would be *wunderbaar*." He cleared his throat. "Wonderful. Thank you."

"You can say *wunderbaar*," she said the word flawlessly. "As a matter of fact, I wouldn't mind learning a little Amish."

Trevor's brow lowered and he looked back and forth from James to Robin. He cleared his throat then pivoted and walked away, joining some of the rest of the group. *Ach*, was his friend purposely giving them time alone?

"I should probably get back to the table to help." She glanced at the other servers at the table, then lightly touched his hand. "Thanks again. I want to hear more of your story later, if you'd like to share it."

James nodded. "Thank you for the food."

When Robin moved back behind the table, he finished his food, tossed his empty plate into the garbage receptacle, and then grabbed his toolbelt. Not many minutes after he resumed working, Trevor joined him.

"I think she likes you." Trevor bumped his shoulder.

"If you're referring to Robin, she's already taken," one of the other workers volunteered.

Trevor glanced at the guy from the base church. Was his name Jimmy? "Are you sure?"

"Yeah, I'm sure. She and Erik have been dating for several months now," Jimmy said.

James's excitement dampened a little. But he hadn't come here to find a girlfriend. He'd come to help people in need. He needed to remember that and keep his focus on the task at hand and not get sidetracked by pretty young women. No matter how friendly they were.

"Too bad, James. I thought she was nice," Trevor said.

"That's not what I came here for. And she is nice. But like Jimmy said, she's already taken." He looked at Trevor. "Let's just focus on our work, *jah*?"

"*Jah*," Trevor echoed.

THIRTEEN

For some reason, Robin had been drawn to the cute Amish guy at the worksite today. And not just because of his peculiar hairstyle. Or the fact that his hazel green eyes had reeled her in.

There had been something about him—something she hadn't been able to identify. An underlying sadness, maybe? Whatever it was, she found herself wanting to learn more about him.

"How'd it go today?" Erik entered the house with Dad, and promptly kissed her on the cheek.

"Good." She smiled. "Are you staying for supper?"

"I was planning on it." He stepped back and studied her. "Unless you don't want me to."

"What's that supposed to mean?"

"Jimmy said you made friends with some guys at the worksite today." Erik frowned, folding his arms over his chest.

"Yeah. So?"

"He said you were flirting with the Amish guy." His eyebrows shot up. "Does that ring a bell?"

She should have known Jimmy would say something to Erik. They'd been best friends since they were all in school together.

"He was just intriguing, that's all." She sighed.

"That's all?"

"I don't know. There was something about him."

"Well, he's not exactly your model citizen. Jimmy said he's homeless."

Robin gasped. "Homeless? How? Why would Jimmy say that?"

"Beats me. That's what that guy Trevor told him. Said he was staying at his house in Indiana before they came down to help."

Now she really wanted to learn more about James. He'd seemed so kind and gentle and likeable. How could a guy like that be homeless? "Did he say anything else?"

"Why do you want to know?" Erik seemed offended. "Don't tell me you want to take him in."

Her heart clenched. "I just...I feel bad for him. Don't you?"

"I haven't even met the guy." He shook his head. "And I don't know how I feel about you talking to him."

Her head snapped back. "What? I'm sorry, Erik. But you will *not* tell me who I can and can't talk to."

"Fine." He leaned close and kissed her cheek. "I'll see you later, then."

Robin scowled at Erik's back as he retreated out the door. Was he throwing a tantrum because he didn't get his way? Or was he just jealous because he'd heard she'd been talking to another guy? Either way, his actions did not sit well with her.

She refused to be micromanaged by *anyone*.

FOURTEEN

"I heard it through the grapevine that you're homeless."

James turned at Robin's words. He hadn't realized that she'd be working on-site today. He glanced around, noting that they were the only two in this area of the house.

"I suppose that is true." He shrugged.

"What do you plan to do?"

He lifted his hammer to the nail on the doorframe. "I don't know. Can't say I've thought much beyond helping out here. *Gott* will provide."

Her smile brightened. "I admire your faith."

He frowned. "My folks don't."

"What do you mean? Is that why you're without a place to live? Did they kick you out?"

"I'm not allowed back on their property unless I agree to go before the church and confess my sin."

Her eyes widened. "What did you do that was so bad?" She shook her head. "There I go again. I'm sorry, it's none of my business."

"*Nee*, it's fine. They do not want me to have *Englisch* friends. My father fired Trevor because he didn't want us spending time together. Coming on this trip was the last straw."

"So, what sin do you have to confess, then? I don't understand."

"I have disobeyed my father's orders in coming here and not breaking ties with Trevor."

"I didn't realize…how old are you?"

"I'm twenty."

Robin frowned. "And you're still expected to do as your father commands?"

James nodded. "Yes."

"Do you have any money saved up? Could you get your own place?"

"No. In our community, we don't get to keep money from our work until after we turn twenty-one. I have very little cash."

A frown settled on her pretty face. "Where did you work before?"

"With my father in his construction business."

"How long have you been working for him?"

"Since I finished school." He set his hammer down

and turned his full attention to Robin.

"So, since you were eighteen?"

"*Nee*. I finished at fourteen. Amish only go to grade eight in school."

"Oh, really? I didn't know that. I guess there's a lot I don't know about that culture." Her frown deepened. "So, you really are homeless, then?"

"I suppose I am. But like I said, *Gott* will make a way." He smiled, hoping to erase the worry behind her eyes.

"Do you have any other relatives that you can stay with?"

He shook his head. "I joined the *g'may*—I became an Amish church member—at seventeen. Since I've left, I will be placed in the *Bann*. Excommunicated. They will not be allowed to have anything to do with me, if that is what my father dictates."

"Oh, goodness, James." Robin touched his forearm and the warmth of her hand seeped through his shirtsleeve. "I'm so sorry. I had no idea."

James was glad to be able to share his story with Robin, but he didn't want her feeling sorry for him. He knew that *Gott* had brought him here and he was confident that *Der Herr* would direct his steps.

There had been something about Robin. He felt like they'd shared a special connection. He wondered if she'd felt it too.

Even now, hours later, he still felt the warmth of her hand on his arm. He liked the feeling very much.

FIFTEEN

"Can he come stay with us?" Robin blurted out the words at the dinner table, causing all eyes to turn in her direction.

"Who?" Mom stared at her.

She'd have to explain the entire situation if they were to agree. "The Amish guy that came to help with the storm cleanup. His name is James. He doesn't have a home anymore."

"For how long?" Dad asked.

"Just until he can save enough money to live on his own, I guess." She went on to explain everything James had told her about working for his father and how the Amish customs fit in to the equation.

By the end of her spiel, both Mom and Dad nodded. And she was pretty sure Mom had tears in her eyes.

"You guys should meet him. He seems so kind and

humble. I think you'd like him." A slow smile spread across her lips.

"Do *you* like him?" Dad's stare pierced her.

"I don't know anyone who wouldn't." She deflected. The truth was, she *did* like him. A lot.

But she had no idea if the feeling was mutual.

"What would Erik think?" Dad voiced her own wonderings.

Robin shrugged. "He'd have to learn to deal with it. For crying out loud, how good of Christians would we be if we won't help a brother when he's down on his luck?"

"Is he a believer?" Mom asked.

"I don't know. I mean, I think he probably is. He talked about God."

"Talking about God doesn't make someone a believer, Robin. You know that." Dad reminded her.

"I know. We didn't really get that far in our conversation, so I can't say for sure." She rubbed her hands together, then looked back and forth at Mom and Dad. "So, what do you think?"

"What does *he* think about it?"

"I haven't mentioned a thing to him. He may not even want to, since it's so far from home." She shrugged. "Either way, though, I really want you to meet him."

"What if you invite him over for dinner tomorrow, then?" Dad suggested.

"He's with his friend Trevor, so we'll need to invite them both."

"Then invite them both." Mom smiled.

The reconstruction of the house they'd been working on had been coming along nicely, to James's thinking. Robin approached just as he'd finished hanging a sheet of drywall.

"Would you and Trevor like to join my family for dinner tonight?"

"We came here with the group, so we don't have our own transportation." Not that James knew how to drive, anyhow.

"Oh, well, my dad or brother could come and pick you up from the hotel."

"That's nice of them." His eyes met hers and their gaze held for a moment longer than necessary. "I'll have to talk to Trevor."

"Okay. Would you let me know before you leave, then?"

"I can do that."

She smiled and his gaze trailed her as she walked off.

A whistle let out behind him. "You've got it bad, my friend."

James turned at Trevor's words. "Did you hear what she asked?"

"Can't say I did."

"She invited the two of us for supper at her folks' house."

Trevor shook his head. "It looks like you're not the only one who's smitten. I don't think her boyfriend's going to like that very much."

James frowned. "I don't want to come between them if they love each other."

"If it was love, my friend, she wouldn't have the hots for you."

"The hots?"

Trevor laughed. "It's an *Englischer* saying. It just means that she has a crush on you."

"We probably shouldn't go to supper, then."

"What do you mean? We most definitely *should* go to supper. Especially since she invited us. It would be rude to say no."

James frowned and then looked to see if Trevor was pulling his leg. "It would?"

"Tell her we'll be there with bells on." Trevor grinned.

"Bells?"

Now Trevor laughed. "Just tell her yes, we'd be happy to join them. Besides, doesn't a homecooked meal sound great?"

"It does."

SIXTEEN

"I heard a car pull up! Are they here?" Robin couldn't quell her excitement. She'd been looking forward to introducing her parents to James, although Dad would have already met him by now, since he was the one who picked James and Trevor up at the hotel.

"Settle down, Robin. I'll go check." Mom looked through the window, then turned to look at Robin. "It's Erik."

"Oh, no. What's he doing here?" He was going to ruin everything.

Mom stopped in her tracks and took Robin's hands, studying her carefully. "Erik is your boyfriend. If you want that to change, you'll need to tell him that."

"Mom, I don't even know if James has feelings for me."

"So, you're just going to keep stringing Erik along

until someone better comes your way? That doesn't sound good, Robin."

"I know. I didn't expect to meet James. But now that I have, I can see that Erik and I aren't right for each other. There's no spark between us."

"A good relationship is more than just sparks, Robin."

"I know that, Mom."

"You'd better get the door."

James had taken his shower in haste but made sure to take his time shaving. He stared at himself in the mirror, wishing he could make his hair appear more *Englisch*. He'd never realized before that he stuck out like a sore thumb, and all of a sudden, he felt self-conscious about it. He frowned at his reflection.

"What's wrong?" Trevor's image appeared in the mirror as he grabbed his toothbrush.

"I look Amish."

Trevor chuckled. "You are."

"Not really." James's frown deepened. "Do you think they'll think I'm weird?"

Trevor shrugged. "Maybe. But who cares? Robin

already likes you. Amish hair and all."

James swallowed. He could hardly believe Trevor's words to be true, but he knew they were, just the same.

"It looks like her dad and brother are here. Are you ready?"

"*Jah*. Do I smell okay?"

Trevor laughed. "You just took a shower. As long as you put on clean clothes, you should smell fine. Come on, lover boy, let's go."

SEVENTEEN

Mom had left Robin and Erik alone in the kitchen, but for the life of her, Robin didn't know how to ask Erik to leave without being rude. She really wished he would, though, before James showed up.

"Dad and Scott went to pick up some of the workers for dinner," she informed Erik, hoping he'd get the hint.

"Oh, I don't mind."

Robin released an internal growl. It wasn't the first time Erik had dropped in for supper unannounced, and it never annoyed her before, but this time it did.

How was she going to offer a place to stay for James if Erik was hanging around? Erik would *not* be happy about this in the least, but it really wasn't any of his business who her family invited to lodge with them.

She attempted to occupy herself by checking on the enchiladas, although they really didn't require checking.

The truth was that she was nervous. If Erik stayed for supper, there was a good chance James would decline their offer to let him live here. And she didn't want to give James any extra reasons to go back to Indiana when his time helping was over.

She needed to gather her resolve. She sighed and clenched her hands.

"Erik, I hate to ask this but, could you leave?"

Erik's gaze narrowed on her and his jaw dropped. "You don't want me to stay for dinner?"

"No." Her hands, now shaky, rested on her hips. Goodness, she felt bad. And terribly rude. "I'm sorry. It's just that we planned to have company and—"

Erik's hands went up. "I get it. Fine. I'll leave."

"Maybe you can join us another night?" She squeaked out.

He hastened to the door but stopped to express his disappointment before stepping outside.

As Robin watched from the window, she cringed when Dad and Scott pulled up with Trevor and James. *Oh, boy.*

Erik halted at his truck, then walked toward Dad's car.

James looked so handsome as he emerged from the vehicle. His eyes immediately strayed toward the house. Had he been searching for her?

Just in case, she stepped beyond the kitchen door and raised her hand in greeting. His face exploded in a full-fledged grin when their eyes met. Robin's heart ping-ponged all over the place. She knew in that moment that James was going to be the man she married. She felt it down to her toes.

His steps hastened as he made his way across the driveway toward the yard. Until Erik stepped in his path.

Oh, dear.

"I'm Erik. Robin's boyfriend."

The last thing James expected to encounter upon his arrival was Robin's boyfriend. The guy looked more than a little perturbed.

James nodded in silent greeting, but he didn't feel inclined to shake the guy's hand. Not that it had been offered to him.

Erik glanced back at Robin, then his stare moved to James. "So, you're the Amish boy she seems to have a fascination with." Erik's eyebrow arched.

The word "boy" hadn't been lost on James, but he chose to ignore it. He had no desire for a confrontation with Robin's boyfriend. Amish folks were non-resistant, and James was no different. He minded his own business and tried not to stick his nose where it didn't belong.

Truly, he just wanted this guy out of his face so he could greet the woman who'd invited him and offer her a proper thank you. If this Erik guy had a problem with him being here, it wasn't James's fault. He'd been invited as a guest.

"Excuse me." When James attempted to step around the guy, he moved in front of him blocking his way. *Ach.*

"Do you think you can just come over here and steal my girl?"

James's heart hammered at the guy's nearness. He'd never had someone in his face like this, and the overwhelming urge for his fist to connect with this guy's gut grew strong. Instead, he stepped away. "I came here for supper."

"Like heck you did." Before he had a chance to block it, Erik's fist slammed against James's jaw.

"James!" Robin shrieked then ran toward them. "Erik, stop!"

Heedless to Robin's words, Erik extended another blow to James's stomach.

James's eyes widened as petite Robin pushed against Erik's chest with what seemed to be all her might. He hadn't budged. The guy had the nerve to laugh at her attempt.

Scott and Robin's father pulled Erik away and not-so-gently encouraged him to leave.

"We're done, Robin!" Erik spit out as he finally got in his truck and peeled out of the driveway.

"Good riddance." Robin shook her head. "I don't know what I ever saw in him."

"Me, neither," her brother Scott agreed.

Pain exploded through James's jaw, and he groaned. He held the side of his face, but it had no effect in causing the pain to subside.

"James, are you okay?" Robin's words emerged breathless. She lifted her hand toward his face, then seemed to think better of it.

His jaw throbbed so badly that he couldn't speak.

"It looks like his jaw might be dislocated." Trevor grimaced. "I don't think he'll be able to eat anything."

"I'm sorry, James. Erik is such an idiot." Tears glistened in Robin's eyes. "Dad, can we take him to the hospital?"

"Sure, honey." A regretful look reflected in Mr. Mills' mien. "Let's go now. Scott, tell your mother to keep supper warm for us. We'll be back as soon as we can. And James might need soup."

James wanted to protest and say that he was fine, but

that would've been a falsehood. And Trevor was right. There was no way he'd be able to eat anything now when he was in pain.

"I don't have any money to pay for a hospital bill," James admitted.

"Oh, don't you worry. You won't be paying a cent of this. This bill is going straight to Erik." Robin's father insisted.

EIGHTEEN

This evening hadn't gone anything like Robin had envisioned. Poor James! She was quite certain being mistaken for a piñata hadn't been part of his vision either. She could wring Erik's neck.

Here James had come all this way to help their community out. Instead, he was in the hospital being examined by a medical professional awaiting a diagnosis.

Robin clasped her hands once again and prayed for a favorable outcome, not caring who in the waiting room might be watching her.

After what seemed like forever, Dad and Trevor entered the waiting room.

Robin couldn't help her worry. "Is he all right?"

"We don't know his diagnosis yet. They're taking x-rays right now." Dad frowned. "The doctor doesn't think it's dislocated."

"He doesn't?" Her heart rate sped up. That was a good thing, right?

"The x-rays will confirm or deny it." Trevor volunteered.

Twenty minutes later, James emerged from the double doors holding an icepack to his face.

The doctor walked beside him and joined them in the waiting room. "He was lucky. No major damage, just some pretty daunting bruises on his face and ribcage. He'll be sore for a few days. He'll want to keep an icepack on his injuries to help with swelling, and I wrote him a prescription for meds if he needs them. Or he can just take some ibuprofen for pain relief. It'll heal up and the bruising should subside within a week or two. No major work for a few days and it's probably best not to make him talk or laugh too much."

"Thank you, doctor," Dad said.

As soon as the man disappeared, Robin melted against James, being careful not to press against his bruised abdomen. "I was so worried about you."

His arms wrapped around her, and his lips grazed the top of her head. "I'm okay."

Robin didn't miss Trevor's raised brow at the sight of their interaction. She reluctantly released James.

"Well, should we go back home and enjoy our

supper now?" Dad grinned. "I don't know about you three, but I'm starving."

James shared a smile with Robin. "I'd love to."

○✎‿

"James, Robin explained your situation to us." A look of sympathy blanketed Mrs. Mills' face as they sat at the supper table. "We're so sorry you've had a falling out with your parents. She tells us you're shunned now?"

He glanced across the table at Trevor, then at Robin. "I haven't been told that officially yet, but yes, they will vote to put me in the *Bann* if I don't go back home and make a kneeling confession soon."

"And his father told him he isn't allowed on the property unless he abandons our friendship," Trevor said. "He thinks I'm a bad influence."

"Are you?" Mr. Mills asked.

"If you consider inviting him to church and youth group and missions trips as a bad influence, then yes." Trevor chuckled. "I'm a very bad influence."

"The truth is they'd rather see me out partying than going to a non-Amish church." James frowned.

Mrs. Mills gasped. "Why?"

"Because when Amish start going to another church, they don't usually return. And they believe that since I've been baptized as an Amish, I will go to hell if I die outside the church." James hoped they weren't right, because he didn't want to go to hell. "If I'm partying, they think I will see I'm wrong and turn back."

"Do you agree with them?" Robin's dad frowned.

"I don't know. I'm not sure what is true and what is not." That was what had been so confusing.

"The Bible states there is only one way to Heaven, and it doesn't mention the Amish church. Or *any* specific church denomination, for that matter," Mr. Mills said.

"It doesn't?" He'd read some of the English Bible, but he hadn't gotten that far in it yet.

"The only way to Heaven is through Jesus Christ." Robin's dad explained. "He is the way, the truth, and the life. He is the only door to Heaven. The door isn't through any church or religious organization. Jesus said, *'No man cometh unto the Father but by me.'*"

James's brow lowered. "How do you go in the door?"

"You simply trust the sacrifice Jesus made when He died for you on the cross. *'If thou shalt confess with thy mouth the Lord Jesus and shalt believe in thine heart that God hath raised him from the dead, thou shalt be saved.'*"

James stared at Mr. Mills. That was it? That was all one had to do to gain eternal life? It almost sounded too good to be true. "Are you sure? Is that what you did?"

"I'm sure. It's what the Bible says. But you should read it for yourself, so that you're sure. Don't just believe because I said it." Mr. Mills grinned. "But to answer your question, yes. It is what I did."

"And what I did," Mrs. Mills said.

"Me too." Robin smiled.

"I did too." Scott agreed.

James stared at Trevor, his brow raised.

"Yes, me too."

James's heart surged. With all these witnesses, he didn't need any more confirmation. But he still wanted to read what the Bible said, as Robin's dad advised. "Will you show me after supper? I'd like to know I'm going to Heaven too."

Excitement exploded from Robin's lips in a squeal and James noticed her eyes misted with tears. She reached across the table and squeezed James's hand.

Ach, he loved the look of pleasure on Robin's face. He wished he could experience that every day of his life.

After supper, James joined Robin's father in the living room. As he showed him the Scriptures he'd mentioned earlier, anticipation filled James's entire being. Before returning to the kitchen for dessert, James had bowed his head and asked *Gott* to save him.

It was a *wunderbaar* feeling indeed knowing he was now on his way to Heaven! And whether he ever turned back to the Amish or not, he was saved for all eternity.

NINETEEN

$\mathcal{E}$ ven though she and Erik had broken up today, even though James endured Erik's wrath and had taken a trip to the hospital, and even though she felt like a ravenous wolf by the time supper touched her lips, today was still one of the most amazing days Robin had ever experienced.

James had trusted Christ to save him!

Now, she was even more sure he was the one.

"Were you going to tell him?" Robin looked to Mom and Dad, then glanced at James.

"Tell him what?" She knew by Dad's tone that he was teasing her. He was purposely drawing this out.

"*Dad.*"

James looked at Trevor and shrugged.

Dad made eye contact with James. "What she's referring to is a discussion we had earlier. About you, James."

"You were discussing *me*?" He chuckled. "Must've been a boring discussion."

"Quite the contrary," Mom said.

"Hey, I feel left out here." Trevor grinned.

"If you must know, we were talking about your state of residence. Or, more specifically, your lack of a residence."

"Dad, you're taking forever." Robin rolled her eyes, then pinned her stare on James. "Would you like to move into our spare bedroom?"

James hadn't been expecting *that*. At all.

He glanced to Trevor, then back at Robin. "What do you mean?"

"You don't have a place to return to, right? Unless, were you planning to move in with Trevor?" She frowned.

"Trevor's place is pretty full right now. I slept on his couch the night before coming here."

"Well, what do you think of our proposition? You're under no obligation to stay for any length of time. We just thought we'd offer since we have a vacant room and Robin said you're basically homeless."

James scratched his chin and looked at Trevor. For sure, he'd miss his friend if he stayed here in Arkansas. "I appreciate the offer." He swallowed. "Honestly, I'd like to think about it and talk to Trevor."

"You're not beholding to me. It sounds like it might be a fresh start for you." Trevor grinned, casting a quick glance at Robin. "You don't have any possessions and you'll need to find a new job anyway. Your parents already cut you off, so what have you got to lose?"

Trevor had a point. James also understood the words his friend hadn't said. If he and Robin were to begin a relationship, he'd need to be in the area.

"How much longer is your crew here?" Robin's father asked.

"A couple of weeks, I think." James looked at Trevor for confirmation.

"If he stays here, you'll need to teach him how to drive a car." Trevor laughed.

James's throat burned. He never thought he'd live so far away from *Mamm* and *Dat*. When would he see them again, if he stayed here? *Would* he see them again?

He'd always wanted to live on a farm in the country. If he and Robin eventually dated and married, would she be willing to move away from her family? It was a lot to think about for sure.

"I want to pray about it," he finally said. Although he was pretty sure he already had his answer. The confirmation was smiling back at him from across the table.

TWENTY

"Man, I can hardly believe Robin's family invited you to live with them." Trevor reclined in his hotel bed and flipped through the muted television channels.

"I know." James plopped onto his own bed. "What should I do? What would *you* do if you were me?"

"Well, you like Robin, don't you?"

"*Jah*. A lot."

"I'd go for it. Like they said, you're not under any obligation to stay. If things go south for you and Robin, you can always move back up to Indiana. You might want to see about finding a job ASAP, though."

"I don't know where I'd work."

Trevor shrugged. "Find a construction crew. They're always looking for good faithful workers and they'd value your work ethic."

"Do you really think I have a chance with Robin?"

Trevor laughed. "Dude, she broke up with her boyfriend over you. And he beat you up."

"*Jah*, I know. I've got the bruises to prove it."

"Well, at least you get out of work." Trevor clicked off the television.

"I don't want to get out of work, though. That's what we came down here for. To help people out. I can't help people if I'm out of commission."

"If you go over to Robin's, I bet she'll fuss over you all day." Trevor's eyebrows raised twice.

James moaned. "I don't want to be fussed over. I want to be a hundred percent so I can do stuff."

"Spoken like a true Amishman. Well, get some rest. I'm sure that will help with your healing."

"I'll have to face Jimmy when I go back to the worksite." James grimaced.

Trevor chuckled. "What? Do you think he'll be upset with you?"

"Probably. He's Erik's best friend."

"He shouldn't be. I mean, *you're* the one who got beat up." Trevor fluffed his pillow, then stuffed it under his head.

"*Jah*, but I'm also the one who strolled into town and stole his best friend's girl."

"You have a point." Trevor yawned. "Don't worry about it, man. God will work it all out. You'll see."

"*Jah*. He will, won't He?" James lay down, then rolled over on his side and moaned. He hoped he'd actually be able to get some rest.

James flipped through the TV channels, hating that he was sitting there alone in the hotel room doing literally nothing.

At least if he'd gone to the construction site he could have been out in the fresh air. But Trevor had pointed out that since he wouldn't be moving around much, he might get a chill, and that would prompt him to get moving which would take his injuries longer to heal. And he was supposed to be icing his injuries.

He briefly wondered if going down to the spa would be a good idea. Whether or not it was, it would at least be something to do. He groaned as he hoisted himself from the bed. His injuries definitely hurt more today than they had yesterday.

After seeing himself in the mirror this morning, he'd decided it was probably a *gut* idea if he came in contact with as few people as possible. Sporting a black and blue face in public tended to draw attention to himself, something he didn't care for. He rather just blend in like a normal person than stick out like a sore thumb. Now, though, he had two strikes against him—his hair and his face. Although, while being Amish, his hair had never bothered him because he looked like everyone else. Now, not so much.

He tried to recall if he'd seen any barbers within walking distance. Wouldn't Trevor be surprised if he returned to an *Englischer* instead of an Amish guy? He smiled to himself. *Jah*, maybe he'd do that today.

A sound at the door drew his attention. Had someone knocked lightly? He looked through the peephole but couldn't see anything.

"Who is it?" he spoke into the door's crack.

"Room service," a voice called back.

He frowned. He hadn't ordered any room service, but maybe Trevor had arranged something. He shrugged and opened the door.

Robin stood smiling on the other side, a tray of food in her hands.

His face brightened. "What is this?"

"Trevor said you were stuck here alone, so I brought you some of the extra food from the worksite."

He was taken aback by her kindness. "*Denki*. You didn't have to do this. It's a long way for you to drive." He took the tray off her hands.

She grinned. "I wanted to. And I figured you could use some company."

"You figured right." Although, the two of them being alone in a hotel room might give people the wrong idea. "Should we go to the sitting area?"

"Sure, we can do that."

He grabbed his hotel key, then they made their way to the elevator.

"I was actually thinking of seeing if I could find a barber." His hand slid through his long hair. "And maybe take a trip to the spa. You didn't happen to bring a bathing suit, did you?" He teased.

She glanced down at her outfit, tugging on her shirt. "Fresh out of bathing suits. I think it might be packed away until spring."

"*Ach*, too bad. It would be nice to have someone to go with." Although that might not be the best idea, considering his attraction to Robin.

"Well, I don't know about the spa, but I could help you find a barber. As a matter of fact, there's a salon just up the road. I'd be happy to go with you if you'd like."

"That would be great. You could help me pick out a new *Englisch* hairstyle."

"Really? You'd want an *Englisch* hairstyle?"

He nodded. "I can't wait to see the look on Trevor's face when he returns to an *Englischer*."

Robin laughed. "He'll be surprised, I'm sure."

TWENTY-ONE

"Wow. I really like your new haircut. It looks great on you." Robin eyed the handsome man in the seat beside her as they headed back to the hotel. So far, she hadn't found anything she didn't like about him.

"Do you think so?" He lifted his hand to his hair, unwittingly drawing her attention to his work-defined arms.

Construction was a good trade for him, she decided with a secret smile. "It suits you."

"It feels so *Englisch*."

"That was what you were going for, right?" She found herself wishing she could run her fingers through it.

"*Jah*, but I'm not used to having so little hair."

She reached over and squeezed his fingers. "You'll get used to it."

"I can't wait until Trevor gets back."

Her smile dimmed a little. She liked Trevor, but she didn't want to think of their special time together ending. "I wish I'd brought my bathing suit so I could keep you company longer."

His smile disappeared. "You're not going to stay until Trevor gets here?"

If only. But if she stayed, she had a feeling he'd want to go back to his hotel room. And that would be a really bad idea if they want to abstain from all appearance of evil. "I'll need to get back home to start on supper."

"I see." An undefinable look flashed across his face. "How long can you stay?"

With you? Forever? "I'm not sure. What are your plans?"

He sighed. "Hide out in the hotel room until this ugliness disappears." He pointed at his discolored face.

"You are anything but ugly, James Stoltz. And looks aren't that important anyhow. It's what a person is like on the inside that truly matters. If a person's heart is ugly, it doesn't matter if they're the most beautiful person in the world on the outside. Nothing is more attractive than a good heart."

He turned in his seat and stared at her.

She glanced back at him and laughed. "What? Why are you looking at me like that?"

"I've never met anyone like you. Actually, I haven't met many *Englisch* girls at all, and certainly never had any real conversations with them."

"Is that bad or good?"

"*Nee*, it's *gut*."

"You're the first Amish person I've met."

"Really?"

She nodded, flipping on her turn signal.

"Am I much different from the *Englisch* boys you know?"

"Yes, most definitely." She studied him as they sat at the stoplight. "Other than your hair, which isn't all that different anymore—your speech, the way you walk, your clothes. And then, I don't know, I guess it's the way you carry yourself. You seem calmer than most people. Relaxed. Humble."

"Wow. You see all that?" His mouth gaped open.

"I do."

"Amish value humility so I'm glad that you noticed it."

"So, you're proud of your humility," she teased, turning into the parking lot.

"*Ach*, I didn't mean that."

She shook her head. She hoped he wouldn't always take her words literally. "I was only teasing. You can add pure and honest to that list too."

"If you knew some of my thoughts, you would not think I am pure." He frowned.

"I didn't say perfect. I know you're not that. Goodness, none of us is." She pulled the car up to the hotel and parked. "I guess I'll let you off here."

"*Jah*. Okay, then." His hand rested on the door handle. "Thank you for taking me to get my hair cut."

"It was a pleasure." She couldn't hide her smile. He looked even more gorgeous than before. "Have you thought any more about the proposal?"

His brow lowered. "Proposal?"

"Staying here in Arkansas for a while."

"*Ach*, that. I have thought a lot about it."

"Good." If he stayed, would they date?

"I haven't decided yet. On one hand, I will be far away from my family." He shrugged. "But I guess it doesn't matter since I can't visit them anyhow." His sober mien endeared him to her even more.

"I'm sorry things are hard with your family. Seriously. I can't even imagine my parents disowning me." Tears pricked her eyes, and she squeezed his forearm.

"That's just the way our people have always done things. It didn't come as a surprise to me."

"I don't think it's right. Do you?" She examined James's stoic features. This young man carried a heavy load on his shoulders, and she longed to help unburden him.

"*Ach*, I'm not sure about my feelings on that yet. It's the way I've always known. I haven't really considered whether it's right or wrong."

"The Bible only speaks of disassociating from believers that are blatantly living in sin."

"That is how I am viewed by them." James frowned. "I broke my vow to the Amish church and to *Gott*, and I am disobeying my folks."

"So, if your parents were to leave the Amish, and you had stayed Amish, would the church *still* want you to obey them?"

"No, because my folks would be in the *Bann* then."

"It sounds like a person's vow to the church is the most important thing in the Amish culture."

"It's my own fault. I shouldn't have joined when I was seventeen. If I hadn't, I wouldn't be in the *Bann*." As he said the words, Robin felt the regret behind them.

"Why did you leave?"

"I wanted to help with this project, and maybe other projects in the future. I like the idea of helping others who are in need." He glanced at her. "And I know it might sound strange, but I felt like *Gott* wanted me to come here."

"It's not strange to me at all. I don't understand why

your father would be against you coming here to help people. I thought I saw on TV somewhere that the Amish went and helped people in another country. Mexico, I think."

James shook his head. "Those are more worldly Amish. Not our group. We would help our neighbors if they were in need. The group I came here with is *Englisch*, not Amish. My father thought I was spending too much time with *Englischers*."

"But the Bible says we're to go into all the world and preach the Gospel to every creature. If your group isn't doing that, why not join up with another church who is?"

"I don't have an answer for that. That's not how it works where I come from. We do a lot of things because that's the way they've always been done. We don't associate with a lot of others—not even many other Amish groups."

The thought baffled Robin. She had never realized how isolated a religious group could be here in America, which made her wonder. "Would *I* be permitted to visit your church?"

His eyes grew wide. "You?"

She chuckled at his shocked expression. "I would like to see what it's like." One thing she did know was that they didn't usually meet inside of a church building but gathered in houses and barns.

"We have never had an *Englischer* come to our church. I don't think the leaders would allow it."

She couldn't imagine not being allowed to attend a church service. "Never? I was sure I read something about a non-Amish person visiting an Amish church and they preached some of the sermon in English so the visiting member could understand."

"Maybe you did. I'm not aware of how other faster Amish do things." He shrugged. "But *our* leaders would probably ask an *Englischer* to leave. Besides, it would not benefit them because our services are not in English, and I don't think that will ever change."

"Oh, I hadn't realized that. That's too bad." Robin's enthusiasm deflated. "It sounds like every Amish church makes their own rules, maybe?"

"*Jah*. It is called the *Ordnung*. And we rely on tradition. We believe the old ways are best." He nodded.

"Do some other Amish churches have their entire services in English, then?"

James shrugged. "I wouldn't know. I have only been to my church."

"Would your parents be against you going to another church—another Amish church that does missions outreach?"

"They would not allow it."

"Do you think your group is stricter than most groups?"

He smiled. "We would say the worldly Amish aren't really Amish because they are not keeping with the old ways."

"Now that *does* sound prideful." Robin laughed.

"I never thought about it like that, but I guess it does, huh?" James chuckled.

"I don't know. I'm not judging them. The Bible says we're supposed to work out our own salvation with fear and trembling. It's not my place to speak against others—unless, of course, they believe something that goes against Scripture."

"But it does go against what I read in the Bible. I had never heard that one could go to Heaven by simply believing in Jesus. It was not taught in my Amish church. I heard a lot of preaching about keeping the Amish *Ordnung*, though." Sorrow flashed across his features. "I am sad that my folks don't know the way to Heaven. Like someone said earlier, the Amish church isn't even mentioned in the Bible. Jesus is the way. Not the Amish."

"Have you thought about talking to your parents and sharing the Gospel with them?"

He grimaced. "I could try, but since they don't want me on their property, it would probably be best if I would write them a letter."

"I think that might be the best idea. Who knows? Maybe they would respond favorably."

He shook his head. "I don't know. My father was voted minister last year. I think that because he is a minister, he feels like he has to be even more strict with me. He's setting an example for the rest of the community." James frowned. "And soon, he could be the bishop."

She glanced out the car window as a young family passed by, then entered the hotel. "How is he stricter compared to other members?"

"Usually, when a person is in the *Bann* they can live at home. They are just not allowed to share meals or receive anything from a member in good standing. They must eat at a table apart from everyone else and not speak much to others. They would not be able to shop at a member's store or have fellowship with other brothers and sisters in the *g'may*—the church."

She sighed. The hopelessness seemed like it would be overwhelming. She couldn't imagine being emotionally manipulated into having to think and act a certain way. "That's sad. That might be worse because you'd have to deal with it day in and day out."

"I think that's the idea. It is a call to repentance—a daily reminder that you are not living according to the Amish ways."

"So, maybe it's a blessing that your parents won't let you live at home."

"I wouldn't have come if I did not think it was *Gott* who wanted me here." He caught her eye and reached over the seat, then tucked a strand of hair behind her ear. "I'm beginning to think that maybe He had more planned for me than what I thought."

Robin's insides warmed at what he might be insinuating. "Do you think God planned for the two of us to meet?"

"Seems that way. I wouldn't have met you had I not come here with Trevor's church."

Her heart hammered in her chest. She wasn't sure about how the Amish felt about physical contact, but she knew that if he were to lean across the console and kiss her right now, she'd happily kiss him back. "Do you feel like there's a special connection between us?"

"I do…"

"I think I hear a "but" behind your words."

"If we were to be together—to marry—I could never go back to the Amish." He stared straight ahead and swallowed hard. "I would have to be sure."

"Do you think you might eventually go back? Because I wouldn't want to keep you from ever seeing your family again." Only now did Robin realize the enormity of what dating James would mean, and the sacrifice he'd be making for her.

She got the feeling the Amish didn't believe in casual dating. Her heart ached at the thought of not getting a chance to date the most wonderful man she'd ever met. Was it possible to fall in love with someone this quickly? Because she was quite certain it was more than just feelings and attraction. James Stoltz held her heart in his hands, and he probably didn't even realize it.

"That's just the thing. I don't know. I don't think that I would go back because then I'd have to give up my English Bible."

Robin frowned. "Wow. They won't even allow you to have an English Bible? Your group must be *really* strict."

"Maybe some worldly Amish do, but not our community. And I'm certain *Dat* and the other leaders would disagree that you don't have to be part of the Amish church to have hope of Heaven. I have a feeling that if I did go back and try to tell people about only believing in Jesus that I would just be put under the *Bann*. There wouldn't really be a point to it."

"If you decide not to stay here, what would you do?"

"I'm just taking one day at a time. I'd like to talk to Trevor about it because, if I did go back, I'd probably be staying with him. I'm not sure how his family would feel about that because it would be a while before I could save up enough money to get a place of my own and a car and all that." He blew out a breath. "*Ach*, I never thought I'd be thinking of getting my own car. It's a crazy thought."

She laughed. "Yeah, I couldn't imagine learning how to use a horse and buggy either."

"I'd like to see that."

Their eyes connected, and he leaned slightly toward her. Her pulse raced when she noticed desire in his eyes.

"I might—*ach*, I should let you go."

Her anticipation plummeted when James moved back.

In a sudden rush, he stepped out of the car. "Thank you again for taking me."

"You're welcome. Be sure to ice your injuries so you'll get better soon." She waved to him as he shut the door, then she watched the man of her dreams disappear inside the hotel.

Yes, James Stoltz was definitely the one.

TWENTY-TWO

The moment Trevor walked through the door, James knew that his friend suspected Robin had visited.

"All right, dude. Spill it." Trevor's grin widened, then he finally noticed. "Whoa! Your hair. Did she talk you into getting a haircut?"

"It was my idea."

"Dude, you look like us *Englischers* now."

"That's what I was hoping for. Although it feels weird." His hand feathered through his hair again. How many times had he touched it since it had been cut? "Does it look okay?"

"It looks great." Trevor squeezed his shoulder. "So, tell me. Did you kiss her?"

He laughed. "*Ach*, I wanted to."

"But you didn't."

James heard the disappointment in his friend's tone,

but he didn't feel bad for not seizing the opportunity. Love was patient, wasn't it? "I don't know how she would feel about it."

"There's only one way to find out."

"Maybe I should have asked her."

"You could, but I think most girls like it when you're spontaneous about it."

Spontaneous? "I'm not sure I know what that means."

"Just do it. If she doesn't want you to, she'll let you know."

"She will?"

"If she doesn't return the kiss, then she's probably not ready for it."

"She looked like maybe she wanted me to kiss her, but I didn't want to assume."

"Then you probably should have asked or just done it."

"Maybe I'll do that next time." His face warmed as he thought of kissing Robin. *Ach*, it would be a dream. He was nervous just thinking about it, though.

"Just remember, once you cross the line of just friends, there's really no going back."

"I wouldn't want to."

"You were right about Jimmy. He complained half the day until I asked him to be quiet about it. Don't worry, everyone will come to terms with it eventually.

Especially if you move in with the Mills." Trevor frowned. "I do worry about gossip, though."

"People always gossip." He'd experienced plenty of that. It seemed nearly impossible to keep secrets in his Amish community.

"Yeah, but if you and Robin are together and you're living under the same roof, some people might misconstrue that to mean the two of you are living together."

"*Jah*, but her folks and her brother will be there too."

"Which is why there's nothing wrong with it, so you shouldn't worry about what other people say. Although, the Bible does say to abstain from all appearance of evil."

James pondered his friend's words.

"But like you said, her parents are going to be in the house too. It's not like you two would do anything with her parents in the house. That would just be awkward."

Heat rushed through James as he realized what Trevor was implying. "*Ach*, I wouldn't…I would wait until we were married."

"Yeah, but you are human and humans tend to get carried away when they're in the heat of the moment. It's best not to trust yourself alone with her. Like if her parents were to go somewhere and the two of you stayed home alone. One thing can lead to another pretty quickly."

Ach. James got the feeling his friend may have been speaking from experience, but he wouldn't ask about something so personal.

TWENTY-THREE

*J*ames tapped his fingers on his pantleg, as he waited for Trevor to don his work clothes.

Two days had been too much. James was ready to go back to work whether he should or not. He'd rather be working in pain than not working at all. Besides, between his ice packs and his trips to the hotel's spa, his pain was now minimal.

Not only that, but if he'd gone to work the second day, he could have seen Robin during their lunch break. He didn't understand how he could miss her so much already. He'd just seen her the day before yesterday.

"I'm glad you'll be working with us today. It hasn't been the same without you there." Trevor tugged his work T-shirt on.

One good thing about James being off was that he'd had a chance to wash their extra sets of work clothes. "*Jah*, me too. I've been going crazy here."

"Do you remember Patti?"

"One of the workers at the site?"

"Yeah." By Trevor's silly grin, James guessed he had a crush on the young woman. "We've been getting to know each other."

"And?"

"I wish I could stay here in Arkansas with you so I could date her."

"That would be amazing. I'd love it if you could."

"I don't think I have enough saved up to rent a place yet, and all my stuff is back home. I was thinking that maybe I could go back and work for a while so we have enough for a deposit and the first month. I'm not sure if they'd rent to us if we don't have jobs here, though."

"I'm going to ask Robin's father if he knows of someone who needs construction workers. If I can start working once our church project is done, then I can start saving money too."

"Then maybe your job history will help us get a place." He caught the excitement in Trevor's voice.

"It sounds like a *gut* plan."

"Who knows? We might both find us wives. I wonder if Patti and Robin are good friends."

"They did talk to each other at the site, but I think Patti might go to a different church."

"If we double date, they'd probably become fast friends." Trevor grinned.

"Maybe." James's lips twisted. "How do *Englischers* date?"

"We will usually go somewhere. Like, to the movies or maybe ice skating and then go out to eat."

James's excitement deflated. "I don't think I'd have enough money for all that."

"Maybe we can do something less expensive, then? Girls usually like picnics, but it's a little cold out right now for a picnic. We might need to get creative, but I'm sure we can think of something that wouldn't cost a lot."

"*Jah.* Okay." Although he had no clue what it would be. In his Amish community, it had been so simple— enjoy singings and games and snack with the other *youngie*, then take a *maedel* home in your buggy and spend the evening together. No fancy supper or movies or anything was expected. "I have an idea. What if we made a game night with snacks and such?"

"That's a great idea. Another thing is we can maybe watch a movie at home with popcorn and treats."

James nodded, his excitement returning. "I don't think we have to spend a lot of money to have a *gut* time."

"You're right. We don't. And I'm thinking the girls

might even like that better than going to a theater. It's more personal and you can get to know each other better, I think."

"*Jah.* Hopefully, Robin's follks won't mind if we use their house." James's lips turned downward.

"Why don't you talk to Robin?"

All of a sudden, his palms grew sweaty. "Okay." He blew out a breath. "We haven't really…I mean, we both know that we like each other. I'm just not sure where to go from here. I don't want to ask her on a date and have her thinking we're going to go out somewhere nice and I'm not able to take her. You know what I mean?"

"Well, you could always ask her what *she* thinks. Tell her that you'd love to take her out someplace fancy, but you're not in the position to do that right now. Then ask her if she has any ideas of things you can do to spend time together."

"That might work. I'll have to remember all that." He fastened the shoelaces on his work boots.

Trevor opened the door to exit their hotel room. "We better get a move on before the bus leaves without us."

TWENTY-FOUR

*J*ames hadn't even realized what time it was until he stopped hammering and looked up and noticed he was all alone on the roof. When he stood and glanced over the other side of the house, he saw the lunch crew finishing their setup, and that the other workers, including Trevor, had divested themselves of their toolbelts and gathered around to eat.

He searched until he spotted Robin and caught her eye.

Her smile warmed his insides. "You joining us, Superman?"

"*Jah*, coming." He'd been so busy working that he hadn't heard anyone holler that lunch was ready. They needed one of those bells like *Mamm* had to call *Dat* in when he was working way out yonder.

He quickly descended the ladder and joined the rest of the team just in time for prayer.

He stepped to the back of the line, so he and Robin could eat at the same time. The set-up crew didn't usually take their lunch until all the workers had made it through the line.

"Will you join me?" He eyed Robin from across the serving table.

"I'd be happy to." She smiled back at him.

Ach, James still couldn't get over the fact that she'd broken up with her boyfriend over him. She was more than he could ever hope for in a woman.

Robin followed him with her own plate of food and they sat at one of the lunch tables the crew had set up. "How has work gone today?"

"Pretty *gut*. We've got half the roof shingled. I'm hoping we can finish it today. If we do, then we'll start painting tomorrow."

"Wow. You don't mess around, do you?" She sipped her water. "How are you feeling?"

"Okay, although I know I still look terrible."

"You look amazing." Her cheeks turned pink when she said the words.

He shook his head.

"No pain?" A faint sweet fragrance drifted upward when Robin reached out to touch his face. Her featherweight fingers sent his pulse skittering.

"A little, but I try to ignore it."

"Make sure to ice it when you get back to the hotel tonight." She reminded him.

"I will." How could he turn this conversation around so that he could ask her what had been on his mind all day? "What have you been up to?"

"When I don't come here, I work. I'll need to go back this afternoon." She shrugged.

"What do you do?" He took a bite of his sandwich. Why did it seem like Robin's sandwiches always tasted better than the ones he made for himself? The flavors seemed to explode in his mouth.

"I do temporary work at a local events venue."

His lips twisted and his eyebrow shot up. "I have no idea what you just said." He chuckled.

"Okay, so when different concerts come to town— say, like Randy Travis coming next week—I might do anything from selling tickets at the booth to distributing event posters around town."

"*Ach*, I didn't realize such jobs existed."

She shrugged. "Well, someone has to do it."

"Do you enjoy it?"

"For the most part, I do. But what I really like about it is the perks." She giggled at his expression. "I'm sorry. I know I'm probably speaking a foreign language to you. What I mean is that I can usually get free concert tickets. Or if it's something else—like the circus—I can usually go for free if I want."

He nodded. "That sounds nice."

"Have you ever been to a concert?"

"*Nee.*"

Her face lit up brighter than he'd ever seen. "Would you like to go to a country music concert with me?"

The side of his mouth creeped upward. "Are you asking me on a date?"

"Yeah, I guess I am."

"I'd love to. Although, I'm afraid I won't know any of the songs."

"Well, then, it looks like I've got my work cut out for me. Can you come over tonight?"

Another date? He couldn't hide his pleasure. "I'll have to talk to Trevor."

"You can invite him too." She glanced to where Trevor was sitting next to Patti. "It looks like he may have made a new friend."

"Do you know Patti?" As he said the words, Trevor and his lunch companion left the table, walked to the trash receptacles, and dumped their plates.

"We've spoken a few times, but I don't know her well. She seems nice."

"*Gut.* Trevor really likes her. We've been talking about…I'd better just tell you all about it tonight."

They both glanced around and noticed they were the

only two still eating.

"Yeah, I guess we'd better hurry up and eat before you have to go back to work."

They both finished their lunches, but not before he reached across the table and stroked her hand. "Thank you. I really appreciate it."

"It wasn't just me. The team worked together." They both stood from the table, trash in hand.

"I meant for everything. For becoming my friend. For inviting me to go to the concert and to your house. For including my friend Trevor. You are so thoughtful."

She stepped close and lightly grazed his cheek with her lips. "Thank you."

He stood speechless, wondering if anyone else had seen their interaction.

"Well, we'd better get back to work. I'll swing by and pick up you and Trevor after I get off work. And I'll let Mom know you're coming for supper."

After they said their goodbyes, James was even more convinced Robin was the woman *Gott* had chosen for him. He couldn't wait to see what the future held.

TWENTY-FIVE

Tonight was the night, Robin decided.

The night when she and James would take their relationship to the next level.

The night that they'd share their first kiss.

But there was one little problem. Okay, maybe two. How would they find time alone together? And how could she get James to initiate the kiss?

She already knew he wanted to. That part wasn't the problem. She'd seen indecision war in his eyes the other day and she realized that he wasn't sure if it would be appropriate to cross the line.

Aside from outright asking him to kiss her—which she certainly did not want to do—how could she let him know kissing her was okay?

Then a disturbing thought occurred to her. What if his Amish community didn't allow kissing prior to marriage? Had that been why he hadn't kissed her?

And if it was, did she have the patience to wait that long?

"I can't believe you scored tickets for a Randy Travis concert. Randy Travis!" Trevor squeezed James's shoulder. "You're right. I think you meeting Robin must've been of God."

"Is Randy Travis a Christian too?" James eyed his friend.

"I'm not sure. I think so. Maybe." Trevor glanced at James as he towel dried his hair. "Have you really never heard any of his songs?"

"Not that I know of."

"Not even 'Forever and Ever, Amen'?"

James shrugged. "I don't know. The title doesn't ring a bell."

A smile spread across Trevor's entire face. "Then you're in for a treat."

James's hand feathered through his short hair. "You ready to go? Robin should be here any time."

"Yep."

As if on cue, a knock sounded on the hotel door.

"Thank you for supper. It was very *gut*." James truly meant the words. Spaghetti was one of the foods *Mamm* never made because *Dat* had never been big on pasta. James happened to love pasta.

"You're welcome, James." Robin's mother extended a kind smile as she helped her daughter clear away the dinner dishes.

James truly enjoyed Robin's entire family. Scott had asked Trevor to join him in a game of Battleship as soon as supper ended. James got the feeling Scott had suggested that so Robin and James could have some time alone. He appreciated the gesture.

"Mom, I'll do the dishes later. James and I are going for a walk." Robin glanced at James and nodded toward the door.

James followed Robin outside into the brisk fall air. "I'm glad I brought my jacket."

Robin's family lived in a suburban area, but each house looked like it sat on two acres. As they walked along the fenced-lined driveway, he reached for her hand.

"Your hands are cold. Do you want to go back and get some gloves?"

"Nah, I think I'll be fine."

He took her hand between both of his and rubbed a little warmth into it, then switched places and did the same thing with her other hand. "Is that better?"

"A little, although, I'm not sure how long it will last."
She shivered.

He stopped walking and opened his jacket. "Come here."

She moved close.

"Slip your arms around me." When she did, he could feel her cold hands through his shirt. He wrapped both arms around her and pulled her to him and she rested her head against his chest. The sensation felt downright heavenly.

They stood there in silence for several minutes as her breathing slowed and a sigh released from her lips. "I love this," she murmured against his chest.

"You do?"

She nodded.

"*Gut.* I do too."

The moment she smiled up at him, he knew it was the right time. He crooked his finger under her chin then leaned down to meet her lips. He took his time. His kiss was slow and purposeful, but he restrained the passion burning in his chest.

He hadn't wanted it to end, and by her response, she didn't either. He reluctantly stepped back before their kisses could escalate to the next level.

She stared into his eyes, making him feel like he was

the best thing that had ever happened to her. "That was perfect. You're perfect."

"*Nee.* Not even close."

"No, I mean you're perfect for me."

"I don't feel *gut* enough for you and your family."

She gasped then leaned back. "What are you talking about?"

He shook his head and stared off into the dark pasture. "I don't have much to give. I have no money or possessions. I don't know how to drive a car and I don't know much about being an *Englischer.*"

She reached up and turned his face toward hers. "Look at me." His eyes linked with hers. "None of that matters to me. Or my family. We understand where you've come from, and nobody expects you to be something you are not. And we certainly don't expect you to become an automatic millionaire.

"What we do see is that you are compassionate and honest and kind and a hard worker. Those qualities are worth so much more than having money or knowing how to drive a car. Do you understand?"

"Maybe, but I still feel inadequate."

"That's your humility shining through again. I don't want you walking around with an inferiority complex, though."

"I'm not sure I know what that means."

"Humility is honorable, but you shouldn't devalue yourself. You are precious because you belong to God. You are a child of the King of Kings and LORD of Lords. And if anyone is inadequate, it is me. You are so much more noble than I am."

"Now, who has a complex?" He teased.

"I speak the truth, though."

"I think that maybe we can both learn from each other." He rubbed her back as she leaned against his chest again.

"Can we just stay like this forever?" When she moved back to look at him, tears shimmered in her eyes.

Ach. "Is something wrong?"

"I hope we never have to be apart. Please say you're staying here in Arkansas."

"I'd do anything you asked of me, Robin Mills." His hand moved to caress her soft cheek.

She squealed.

"But I did want to talk to you about something," he said.

"What?"

He held her close, but the house provided more heat than he could. "Do you want to talk out here or should we go back inside?"

"I think I'm a little warmer now. Why don't we walk?"

"Okay." He slipped his hand in hers as they strolled side by side. "Trevor and I have been talking. He's thinking of moving out here too. He wants to date Patti. Actually, he wants us to double date."

"Really? Aww, that's cute."

"He's thinking of going back to Indiana to work a little while until he saves up enough money to rent an apartment or house. I don't want to live in your folks' house any longer than necessary, so I want to try to find a job once we're done with the mission work. Then, when Trevor moves over here, he and I can be roommates."

She nodded. "That sounds like a solid plan."

"But one of the issues is he would like us to go on a couple of dates before he goes back. Since neither one of us have all that much extra money, we were hoping that maybe your folks would let us have a game night here as one of the dates."

"Oh, I'm sure they wouldn't mind." Her grin widened. "That sounds like fun."

They made a U-turn in the driveway and began walking back toward the house.

He was thankful that she liked his ideas. "We were thinking we could do a home movie night for a date too."

She shook her head. "See? That's what I love about you."

"What?"

"You're resourceful. If there isn't a way, you will try to make a different way that works for you."

He shrugged. "I can't take all the credit. Some of the ideas were Trevor's."

"I'm glad he wants to move down here too. I can see that you two are good friends and it's important to have friends you can trust." She tugged on his hand as they neared the house. "Come on, let's go listen to some twang."

"Twang?"

"Country music. My Randy Travis CD, to be more specific." Her smile brightened her face.

He took a deep breath. Hopefully, he'd like this music. But he knew that even if he didn't, he'd happily go to the concert to be next to Robin all night.

TWENTY-SIX

The next two weeks flew by, and James hated to say goodbye to Trevor, although he took comfort in the prospect of seeing his friend again in a couple of months, if the Lord willed.

They'd only gotten to enjoy one double date, but Trevor and Patti seemed to hit it off. Trevor said they'd made plans to call each other and maybe even send a letter or two while he was in Indiana.

Which reminded James of the letter he'd sent to his folks a couple of weeks ago. In his letter, James had poured out his heart. He'd told his folks about meeting Jesus and how he'd felt *Gott's* hand on him. He'd written all about Robin and the relationship they'd established and about their desire to serve *Der Herr* together.

For several days, he'd wondered what *Mamm* and *Dat's* reaction had been. Until his letter returned unopened, accompanied by letters from both *Mamm* and *Dat* begging him to return home and repent of his sinful ways before he died and faced hell fire. Fortunately, since he'd accepted Jesus' payment for his sins, he knew he was no longer in any danger of hell.

Robin's family pledged to pray for James's folks and that they would find Jesus. Every day he spent with Robin's family had been a blessing.

But he missed Trevor something wonderful. He looked forward to the day that his friend would return and they would set up an apartment and become roommates again.

His relationship with Robin grew stronger every day, along with their attraction to each other. James wasn't so sure that living in the same house with her after a month was such a *gut* idea. Trevor had been right in warning him about temptation. The sooner his friend arrived in Arkansas, the better.

Robin lay awake in her bed with thoughts of James swirling through her mind. Goodness, she couldn't help but love him with everything in her. She could only dream of the day when they'd become husband and wife. But that day was still a long way off—at least a year or more.

She really needed to learn to be patient. Everything was perfect in its time, right? But having him here in the same house was mind-numbingly wonderful. And dangerous, the way her thoughts were trending.

Robin listened in the dark. The door to James's bedroom had just closed, so it would be safe to venture across the hallway in her nightgown.

Just as she reached the bathroom door, James stepped out. *Oh my.*

He stood in front of her shirtless in only his boxer shorts. His gaze trailed her nightgown and she swallowed. His eyes lit with desire and his hand grasped hers, then continued upward to her shoulder.

He dipped his head and his mouth found hers. Up until now, his kisses had always been restrained. She'd never felt such passion as he deepened the kiss, pressing her back against the wall next to her bedroom door.

In the next moment, they found themselves reclining against her pillows. Robin's heart beat so hard and fast, she was certain this crazy wonderful feeling must be a dream. God help her, she desired James with everything in her.

Robin's heart—and their progress—thudded to a

stop when the light switch flipped on. *Oh no!*

"What is the meaning of this?" Dad demanded.

Robin stared at James's bare chest and boxers and bit her lip. Goodness, he was even more gorgeous with the lights on.

Dad's gaze moved to the unfastened buttons on Robin's nightgown and scowled.

Her face burned. She hadn't thought she could get much hotter than a moment ago, but she'd been wrong.

Dad marched over to James, grabbed him by the arm and hauled him to the bathroom. "Turn the shower to as cold as it gets and you stay under it until you've had a chance to cool off, boy."

Robin covered her face. She'd never been so embarrassed in her life. To lose herself in the moment with James was one thing. But to have Dad walk in on them was a hundred times more humiliating.

What was Dad going to do with them?

"Margaret, get out here!" Dad hollered.

Mom rushed out of their bedroom with her housecoat wrapped around her. "What is it?"

"You need to have a talk with your daughter." He huffed, then pointed to the closed bathroom door. "This one is taking a cold shower."

Robin still covered her face when Mom entered her room. "Mom, we didn't…we were just—"

"If I hadn't interrupted them, there's no telling *what* would have happened." Dad snapped. "You." He ordered James as he stepped out of the bathroom wrapped in a towel and shivering. "Go put your clothes on then meet me in the living room."

Oh, goodness. Poor James.

A few moments later, the four of them—Robin, James, Mom, and Dad—sat in the living room. Robin and James were on opposite sides, both staring at the floor.

"Here's how this is going to work." Dad paced the floor. "Either you two are getting married tomorrow, or we're shipping James back to Indiana. What's it going to be?"

Mom gasped. "Frank!"

"I know what I just saw, Margaret. These two cannot be in the same house together."

James stood from the couch. "We can marry, if that's what Robin wants."

Robin's eyes searched his and her heart flip-flopped. "We can?" She whimpered.

He gave a single nod. She knew he was as embarrassed as she was.

"But you can never be Amish again," she reminded him. As much as she desired to marry James, she didn't want him to regret this decision for the rest of his life.

"I know. It is as *Gott* wills." The love in his eyes was a caress to her soul.

Robin could hardly believe he'd be willing to give up his family forever. For her. Tears burned her eyes and she mouthed, "I love you."

His reciprocating smile was as good as saying, "I love you, too."

"Fine, then. Tomorrow it is." Dad sighed. He pointed to Robin. "You. Lock your door and go to sleep."

She nodded, but hesitated.

Dad's scowl met James. "The next time you touch my daughter, it better be as her husband."

James swallowed. "Yes, sir." His eyes flicked toward her one more time.

"Now, everyone go to bed. Tomorrow's going to be a big day."

As James and Robin stood in front of the preacher, he found himself wishing Trevor could be the one standing by his side instead of Scott. But Scott would have been his second choice.

Robin's closest friend had been out of town, so Patti stood next to her. Since they'd been short on time, it had been decided that Robin would wear her mother's wedding dress. Vintage or not, James couldn't imagine Robin looking more beautiful than she did now.

James had borrowed a shirt and tie from Scott. Although he felt funny in it, his apprehension disappeared the minute Robin's gaze fell on him. He'd caught the look of pleasure in her loving stare, and for the first time, he felt *gut* about wearing the uncomfortable outfit.

Since Robin's parents had saved a lot of money by not having an elaborate wedding, they'd given James and Robin a honeymoon trip to the beach and a nice down payment on an apartment of their own.

When Trevor had learned the news of their nuptials, he'd been shocked. And although their plans to become roommates had changed, his friend was genuinely happy for them. He still planned to move south as soon as he could manage it.

A year later, James and Robin stood next to Trevor and Patti as they said their vows. Grandpa and Grandma Mills had tended to baby Wesley as they enjoyed their friends' special day.

Four years after that, little Randy Travis Stoltz had been born. James and Trevor had established their own successful business, but parted ways when Robin and James decided to move back to Indiana to attempt to reconnect with James's Amish parents.

James had pretty much acclimated to the *Englisch* culture, since he'd been immersed in it day in and day out. Occasionally, he would miss some of the Amish ways. But after seeing how holding on to traditions had separated his family, he was even more grateful for the ones in his life who'd shared the truth of God's love with him.

If only his father could read the verse in Colossians about how God had blotted out the ordinances that were against them and nailed them to the cross. With everything in him, James desired that his Amish parents would come to personally know the Saviour who died for them and experience the freedom he now had in Christ.

TWENTY-SEVEN

After James had finished sharing his and Robin's story with the group—leaving out the most intimate parts—his second daughter-in-law, Holly, spoke up. "Now, I can understand and appreciate Randy's name. Was the concert your first date, then?"

Robin shared a smile with James. "Our first official date."

"So, do you like Randy Travis's music now?" Shannon asked.

"My favorite country singer." Memories of their first concert together filled James's mind. Robin had looked so cute in her cowboy hat and boots.

"I also understand why you guys wanted me and Wesley to get married right away, since that's what Grandpa Mills insisted for you." Shannon and Wesley shared that same look of love that James and Robin had been sharing all these years.

"And I think we turned out all right," Robin said as she sat by his side and intertwined her fingers with his.

"When we stopped by Grandma and Grandpa Stoltz's house the first time and they rejected us, why didn't you decide to move back to Arkansas?" Their youngest son, Randy, asked. That particular sad visit had left an indelible mark on his son's fragile soul. It was something he'd had to work through as an adult.

"Because we were committed to reaching out to your Amish grandparents. We, Grandma and Grandpa Mills, and Trevor's family all agreed to pray for Christopher and Judy. We figured that with all of us lifting our voices to Heaven, God would eventually open their eyes to His truth," Robin said.

"It took a little longer than we'd hoped, but Dad always said God's timing was perfect." James smiled at his folks. There was no greater joy than knowing that his parents had accepted Christ's love gift and now his entire family was on their way to Heaven.

Just then, one of the little ones cried from the other room, prompting Robin's departure, and Jaycee burst through the back door with Brighton on his heels. Both boys carried snowballs.

Before James had a chance to speak, Wesley had shot up from his place on the couch and was ushering the boys back outside. The scene brought back fond memories of his own boys while growing up here and the many Indiana winters they'd weathered as a family.

He surveyed all the blessings packed in the humble home he and Robin—with God's help—had built. Yes, God had been good to them.

EPILOGUE

Christmas Eve had been a surprise in more ways than Wesley could count.

They'd been blessed overnight and had awakened to another lovely snow-covered landscape. He'd never tire of the beauty that accompanied God's paintbrush.

When they arrived at Mom and Dad's house, they'd been shocked to learn that not only had Grandma and Grandpa Mills come to visit, but they'd brought along Dad's longtime friend Trevor and his wife, Patti.

Then Grandma and Grandpa Stoltz had arrived.

Tears were shed as Dad introduced his Amish parents to Mom's parents for the first time. Grandpa Stoltz hadn't even known that Dad's friend Trevor had moved down to Arkansas all those years ago. They enjoyed catching up.

And while all these things were exciting in

themselves, there were yet more blessings to be realized.

Randy and Holly welcomed their brand-new baby boy to the family—little Jonah would make a fine playmate for Wesley and Shannon's Noah as they grew up together.

Last but not least, Grandpa Stoltz announced that the leaders and members of the *G'may* had voted to lift the *Bann* on Dad, which meant they could openly fellowship. And Grandpa Stoltz had also been reinstated as the district's Amish bishop. Grandpa Stoltz determined that he would lead their people by God's Word and point their Amish district to their wonderful Saviour who'd been born in a manger over two thousand years ago.

Wesley determined that this was without a doubt the best Christmas ever, but he still wondered if any of this would have taken place if it weren't for Jaycee mistaking Grandpa Stoltz for "Santa" several years ago.

God's ways would never cease to amaze him.

THE END

It's not too late to subscribe to my newsletter! Get a FREE Amish story as my thank you gift when you sign up for my newsletter here: www.jenniferspredemann.com

COMING 2023 (Lord Willing)

The Amish Courtship Series

Preorder ***A Widower's Amish Courtship*** now!

If you haven't read the AMISH COURTSHIP SERIES,
you'll want to continue reading with

A Forbidden
Amish Courtship

Amish Courtship Series

Jennifer Spredemann

© 2021

ONE

As much as Sammy Eicher hated this place, one would think he'd go to great lengths to avoid it. One would *think*. Not something he'd been doing much of lately, evident by his circumstances.

Endless moments ticked by in silence as Sammy's frustration mounted and he stared at the three white walls surrounding him. The small cot beneath him groaned in protest when he leaned forward to get comfortable. *Comfortable? Not probable in this wretched cell,* he mused.

The clanking of metal compelled him to glance up to identify who stood behind the barred iron door, now sliding open. Sammy swallowed hard. *Dat.*

Although seeing *Dat* in this place was difficult, gratitude filled him. He could always count on his *vatter*.

Dat's eyes didn't lift to meet his. If they had, Sammy

was certain he would have read the disappointment and shame in their depths. Again.

Unlike Sammy's father, the jailor's scornful gaze didn't hesitate to meet Sammy's. "I don't know why you keep bailing this boy out, Eicher."

Dat's brow puckered as he studied the jailor momentarily. "He's my *sohn*."

"Yeah, well, if it was *my* son, you bet I'd have his hide the minute we got home."

Sammy scowled at the jailor, who smirked in return.

"*Kumm*, Samuel." *Dat* still hadn't looked his way.

The jailor stood to the side as Sammy stepped out of the cell and followed *Dat* down the long corridor. *Dat's* heavy footfalls drowned out every other sound.

If there was one thing Sammy detested, it was disappointing his father. Especially since *Mamm* passed on.

"You'll need to pay to get your car out of impound." The jailor gestured to the female clerk. "Peggy here will get you squared away and make sure you get your belongings."

An hour later, surrounded by his *vatter* and four siblings, Sammy sat down to supper. *Dat* must've asked the *kinner* not to say anything about his stint in jail, because not one of his siblings mentioned it. He suspected he and *Dat* would have a talk later. *Dat* had never been one to deal with the *kinner* while an audience was present, it had always been one on one, for which Sammy was grateful.

"I forgot to mention, there was a *maedel* that stopped by earlier." *Dat's* frown deepened.

Sammy glanced at his siblings, then back to his *vatter*. "Amish?" He was quite certain he already knew the answer, which was why *Dat's* mouth tugged downward.

Dat shook his head ever so slightly, probably in hopes the *kinner* wouldn't know Sammy had been dating an *Englisch* girl. *Dat* had been aware of it for some time now. He'd briefly expressed his disappointment once.

Sammy had never been one to toe the line, although he did respect his *vatter's* opinion on such matters. This time, however, Sammy was too involved to just give Miranda up. He knew he'd eventually need to make some hard decisions, but he wasn't ready to fully commit yet. Not to Miranda and the *Englisch* world, and not to the *Ordnung*.

To tell the truth, he was a little afraid of making the wrong decision. He knew that if he committed wholly to the Amish lifestyle, he'd have to give up many of his favorite things. Namely, his car and his girl. It would be quite handy to be able to look into the future and see what it held if he followed each path.

But that wasn't how life worked. There was no easy road.

"She left an envelope for you," *Dat* set his fork down and stared at him. Although *Dat* had never outright told him not to date an *Englisch* girl, his disapproval was clear.

"Where is it?" Sammy's chair slid back with a push of his feet on the wood floor. He nearly sprung upward, then thought better of it when he noticed *Dat's* frown deepen even more. *Ach*, he hadn't been accustomed to waiting on a prayer after his meals in jail. He tapped his foot, as he attempted patience he wasn't feeling.

Dat's gaze flickered toward the *kinner*, then came to rest on him. "It can wait. Why don't you finish your meal, *sohn*? Your *schweschdern* worked hard to prepare your favorite. It's *gut*, ain't not?"

His father's calming tone must've held some special power, because it always had a way of soothing Sammy's nerves.

Sammy suddenly recognized what was in front of him and a pang of regret clenched his heart. Sure enough, he'd failed to thank his sisters for the potpie, that was probably delicious. Thus far, he'd only nibbled on the generous portion he'd been served. His thoughts had been so preoccupied with everything else, that he hadn't even noticed what had been set before him.

When he lifted his eyes, neither *schweschder* dared glance his way. He cleared his throat. "Anne, Charlotte, *denki* for the meal."

They briefly looked his way and nodded.

He shoveled in another bite. "It's very *gut*."

A sad smile lifted the corner of Anne's mouth. What was his *schweschder* thinking? Did she believe he was about to jump the fence? Were she and her beau struggling? He'd never been *gut* at figuring out women.

Which made his thoughts veer back to the letter from Miranda that *Dat* mentioned. He couldn't recall her ever writing him a letter. She hadn't visited him in jail this time. Not that the fact should alarm him. She'd said as much last time he'd been incarcerated. Still, concern prickled his skin.

Although she was *Englisch*, she didn't like his rebellious side. She claimed he took too many risks. But that hadn't stopped her from joining in on some of his risky behaviors. He'd first met her at an *Englisch* party, after all. He'd thought her attractive from the get-go, but it was his *Englisch* friend's commendation that she was an easy yes that gave him the confidence to ask her out. His friend had been right.

They'd been dating about six months, but he had no idea where they were headed. Every time he thought about a future with Miranda, doubts filled his mind. While there were many things he enjoyed in the *Englisch* world, he couldn't quite see himself fitting in entirely.

He had friends who had jumped the Amish fence and they often spoke of missing home and how foreign the *Englisch* world was. They said *Englischers* spoke about things that they had no clue about, which made them feel unlearned. Sammy understood that from just hanging out with Miranda and her brother. They'd talk about television stars and events and places they'd learned about in school and whatnot. Sammy would listen politely, but the conversation always went straight over his head. But he didn't mind being ignorant about stuff that didn't matter. He'd rather be smart in practical things.

Sammy knew he wanted a *fraa* who knew how to cook, sew, and do all the other things Amish women learn growing up. Miranda didn't totally lack domestic skills, but she was a long way off compared to his Amish *schweschdern*. He also needed a partner who knew him well and would work alongside him, if need be. He just wasn't sure if Miranda, or any *Englisch* girl, was the right person.

"You gonna eat your food, *sohn*, or just play with it all evening?"

Sammy's head snapped up at *Dat's* comment. "*Ach*, sorry, *Dat*. I guess I just have a lot on my mind right now."

"Better see to your supper."

Sammy nodded, then trained his eyes on his food. He glanced up at his *schweschdern's* discouraged faces and determined not to be a burden to them. Perhaps he'd pitch in and offer to help with dishes tonight.

Sammy stared down at Miranda's brief letter.

> *Dear Sammy,*
> *We need to talk. Call me when you get out of jail.*
> *Miranda*

Sammy tossed the note into his desk drawer, then joined his father in the living room. "I need to go out, *Dat*."

Dat frowned at him over his newspaper. "I thought you would be helping with the chores this evening."

"*Jah*, I plan to. I just need to run out to the phone shanty. I shouldn't be long."

"Alright, I'll expect you back soon then." As *Dat* set the newspaper to the side, Sammy recognized the photo on the front page.

Ach. Did *Dat* know that was him and Miranda in the picture? Sammy's cheeks burned at the thought of his family viewing the photo of the two of them—him shirtless with the word "peace" painted across his chest and Miranda in her bikini top—at the concert rally they'd attended before he'd been arrested. *Dat* would surely think Sammy was on his way to hell—if he didn't already.

Maybe he should try to smuggle the newspaper out of the room after *Dat* retired for the evening. Too bad he couldn't get it now, although there was a *gut* chance *Dat* had already seen the front page. *Dat* was quite thorough when it came to reading his newspapers.

"We need to talk later," *Dat's* voice called out just before Sammy stepped out the door.

Talk, indeed. Sammy expected as much. It wasn't something he was looking forward to either. He knew *Dat* would be right, as usual, and his words of wisdom weren't always comfortable to hear. *Dat's* words always had a way of aiming straight toward Sammy's heart.

Sammy hustled out to the phone shanty, not willing to make *Dat* more disappointed in him than he already was. He stepped inside the phone booth, planted himself on the chair, picked up the phone's receiver, then dialed Miranda's telephone number.

"Hello," a vaguely familiar male voice echoed through the line.

Sammy heard a giggle. "Give me that, silly." It was Miranda now. "Hello?"

Sammy frowned. He was certain he'd called the phone number that connected to Miranda's bedroom. "Who was that?"

Miranda gasped. "Sammy? Uh...is that you? I didn't expect..." Sammy heard muffled voices, then Miranda was back on the other end. "You're out of jail already?"

Sammy's skin prickled with uneasiness. Something wasn't right. "Obviously." Sarcasm spewed from his lips. "I got your note."

"I just, I didn't expect you to be out this soon."

"*Jah*, you already said that." He frowned. "Your letter said you wanted to talk."

"Yes, but in person. When can you meet me?"

"I don't have my car back yet. I'm going to have to earn some money to get it out of impound. I'll have to bring the buggy." He wrapped his finger with the phone cord, then pulled it out of the coil.

"How about the park? Tomorrow? At ten in the morning?"

He knew the park she'd spoke of well. It was just down the road a couple of miles. They'd once...*ach*, he shouldn't allow his mind to dwell on what they'd done there. He dispelled the memory and cleared his throat. "*Jah*, that should work."

"Okay then." She sounded in a hurry to hang up.

"Miranda?" He spoke with haste.

"Yeah?"

"Who answered your phone?" He couldn't say goodbye without knowing.

"Ah, nobody. See you tomorrow. Bye."

The phone clicked off and Sammy stared indignantly at the receiver in his hand before slamming it down in frustration. Anxiety grew in his gut. If Miranda had been cheating on him…

He suddenly felt nauseous.

TWO

"Is it true, Glen?" Roberta Kauffman couldn't hide her grin if she glued her lips together.

"Is what true?" Her brother sat on the milking stool and pretended to not know what she was talking about.

Roberta planted a hand on her hip and tapped her foot. She shouldn't have to spell it out for her dim-witted *bruder* again. "Sammy Eicher. Is it true he's out of jail?"

"How would I know?" Why was her *bruder* being so *dumm*? Of course, he'd know.

"You're his best friend. If anyone knows, you should." She pinned him with a stare. "Besides, Lena Bontrager saw his *dat* driving down the road and she was pretty sure and certain Sammy was in the buggy too."

"What's it to you, anyhow?"

"Well, I—"

"You still have a crush on him, don't you?" He shook his head. "You'd be better off setting your sights on someone else. Sammy's no good. And besides, he already has an *Englisch* girlfriend." Glen scowled.

"I thought you said they broke up."

"Don't go spreading rumors, *schweschder*." He aimed a teat in her direction and sprayed her with warm cow's milk. "I said they *should* break up. Miranda's too good for Sammy."

"*Ach!*" She wiped the milk from her face. Why did *brieder* have to be so exasperating? "How can you say that about your best friend? And she is *not* too *gut* for Sammy."

Roberta had seen the girl before, and quite frankly, she didn't know what Sammy saw in her. Why, she didn't even know how to dress properly!

Her conscience immediately pricked her. She really should be more charitable toward Miranda. It wasn't her fault she was *Englisch* and didn't know any better.

Her *bruder* laughed heartily. "I think you're just jealous."

"What? She's the last person I'd be jealous of."

"Whatever you say, *schweschder*."

"Sammy's a *gut* man."

"You only say that because you've got blinders on. This is the third time he's been in jail, you know. He's getting a reputation." Glen pointed at her. "And if *Dat* had any idea you have your *kapp* turned toward Sammy, you know he'd forbid it outright."

Roberta frowned. Was she the only one who saw the truth of the matter? It was obvious to her that Sammy Eicher was hurting deep down inside. He only did stupid things because he was grieving the loss of his *mudder* and didn't know how to deal with it.

All he needed was someone to take his hand and show him that it was okay to pour his heart out to *Gott*. He didn't have to be strong all the time or hide behind parties and alcohol and cars. What he needed was right in front of him.

If only…

Ach, her *bruder* was right. She shouldn't be having fanciful thoughts of her *bruder's* best friend. After all, Sammy was three years older than she was. He probably didn't even know she existed as a woman.

Maybe that would change if Sammy began attending the young folks' gatherings again. *Jah*, she'd pray for that.

Available in paperback and ebook APRIL 2023, Lord willing!

Dear Reader,

I hope you've loved reading my Unlikely Amish Christmas series!

I don't know if I'm ready to say goodbye to all those sweet *kinner* and the couples who've shared their stories with us—Shannon and Wesley, Randy and Holly, Christopher and Judy, and now James and Robin. Isn't it amazing how fictional characters can wiggle their way into our hearts?

What a fun and *emotional* series this was to write! Like you and me, each character had their own life issues to work through. I hope you will realize, like they did, that you can trust God to carry you through the difficult times.

And never discount what God is doing with your life. To Christopher, Jaycee mistaking him for Santa had just seemed like a happy coincidence. But we can see now that God had a much bigger plan that included not just them, but many others as well.

Until this life is over, we probably won't realize the impact we have had on others. I want to do all I can to point others to Jesus. How about you?

I know I'm going to miss these characters, but like I've said before, the *wunderbaar* thing about books is that you can go back and visit your favorite characters and places again and again.

If you have completed the series, I sincerely hope it has been a blessing! Thanks for reading.

To GOD be the glory!

Blessings in Christ,
Jennifer Spredemann
Heart-Touching Amish Fiction

P.S. Word of mouth is one of the best forms of advertisement and a HUGE blessing to the author. If you enjoyed this book and/or series, **please** consider leaving a review, sharing on social media, and telling your reading friends.

DISCUSSION QUESTIONS

1. At the onset of the story, the Stoltz family gather to decorate the Christmas tree. If you purchase a fresh Christmas tree each year, when do you buy it? Do you get it from a lot or a tree farm?

2. In the first book in this series, the children place their new ornaments on the tree. Do you have a favorite ornament? How often do you purchase new ornaments?

3. Do you gather with family at Christmastime?

4. When tragedy strikes the Stoltz family, their life is changed forever. Have you had to deal with loss? Do you feel like it changed you?

5. James has a good relationship with his parents until they have a disagreement. Has a disagreement ever separated you from loved ones?

6. Do you feel James was wrong when he went against his father's wishes? Do you think adult children should "obey" their parents?

7. Have you ever had a friend that your parents disapproved of?

8. James was determined to follow God's will even if it went against the teachings of his church. Are you willing to follow God at any cost?

9. When the Mills family hear of James's plight, they're happy to help. Have you ever helped someone out in this same manner?

10. Have you ever been without a home to call your own?

11. Do you believe that God guides us in our daily lives? Can you share an example from your own life?

12. If you enjoyed this story, will you kindly consider leaving a review? Thanks!

A SPECIAL THANK YOU

I would like to express a *special* **thank you** to all my readers, who helped with the names in this book. To readers, **Shannon Spaulding** and **Mary Deighton**, thank you for suggesting the names "Robin" for Wesley and Randy's mom, and "Noah" for Wesley and Shannon's young son. Also, thank you to **Connie Lynch** for suggesting the book's name *Unlikely Season*.

I'd like to take this time to thank everyone that had any involvement in this book and its production, including my Mom and Dad, who have always been supportive of my writing, my longsuffering Family— especially my handsome, encouraging Hubby, my Amish and former-Amish friends who have helped immensely in my understanding of the Amish ways, my supportive Pastors and Church family, my Proofreaders, my Editor, my Author friends, my wonderful Readers who buy, read, offer great input, and leave encouraging reviews and emails, my awesome Launch Team (Cherese Akhavein, Barbara Beechy, Julie Brown, Dawn Crawford, Connie Lynch, Sonja Nishimoto, Michelle Rhoden, Patti Stephenson, Emma Stuck, Lori Wilen, and Kay Wingo) who, I'm confident, will 'Sprede the Word' about *Unlikely Season*! And last, but certainly not least, I'd like to thank my ***Precious LORD and SAVIOUR JESUS CHRIST***, for without Him, none of this would have been possible!

If you haven't joined my Facebook reader group,
you may do so here:
https://www.facebook.com/groups/379193966104149/

Made in the USA
Las Vegas, NV
08 January 2024